Escape Route

Elan Barnehama

Published in North America and Europe by Running Wild Press. Visit Running Wild Press at www.runningwildpress.com Educators, librarians, book clubs (as well as the eternally curious), go to www.runningwildpress.com for teaching tools.

ISBN (pbk) 978-1-955062-43-5
ISBN (ebook) 978-1-947041-75-2

Dedicated to the memory of
my parents, Arye and Bea Barnehama,
who escaped

ACKNOWLEDGEMENTS

To my brothers. Henry Shaw, for whom kindness is a default and generosity a reflex. Jim Farka, who makes triumphs sweeter and setbacks softer. Ritchie Warman, for whom curiosity is an instinct. And Jeffrey Weinberger Winwood, for being in charge of morale. Michael Schoenberg, who seeks joy in everything, real and imagined.

I am thankful for Rhonda Fishman, who appeared and disrupted everything, added adventure to my risky road – and now we are writing new chapters together. Lenny Pearl, musician, chef, nephew, friend, and fellow word traveler. Denise DeNitto Shaw, my insistent reader who is sorely missed. Sarah Catz, baseball geek for whom every pitch matters. Steve and Diane Pessinis, who bring the party wherever they go. June Cuomo, patron saint of optimism and brilliant dinner soirees. Eleni Hatzakis, for her big-heartedness. Kiki Smith, my sister by choice whose life is art. To the original Sage team: Sam, Freddy, Larry, Seth, Mitchel, John, Georgia, Henry, Jimmy, Ritchie, Jeff. And a special thank you to my outstanding editor Benjamin B. White, for his insight, patience, and persistence.

Thanks to my children, Ezra and Rebecca, Arye and Laura, for continuing the story. And Ayla and Elijah who are next.

Thanks to Skip and Barbara Jones and the Fairhope community for the opportunity to be a Wolff Cottage Writer-in-Residence, Fairhope Center for the Writing Arts, where I worked on *Escape Route*.

PREVIOUSLY PUBLISHED PORTIONS OF ESCAPE ROUTE

Thanks to the following journals who published portions of *Escape Route* in somewhat different forms:

- "Radio Days," Entropy Magazine, February 2021
- "Home Team," Boog City Press, October 2020
- "Boston Uncommon," 101words.org., July 2020
- "Life Is Groovy," Red Fez #136, June 2020
- "Outlaws," Drunk Monkeys, April 2020
- "Raining In The Holy Land," JewishFiction.net, September 2018
- "Just Be," Anthology of Stories, Volume 2, Running Wild Press, March 2018

"A friend may well be reckoned the masterpiece of nature."
Ralph Waldo Emerson

I

1968

THE TIMES THEY ARE A-CHANGIN'

"Revolution is in the air," Ali said, "and it smells good."

She was leaning against my bedroom door the night before my Bar Mitzvah. I was in my room practicing my part of the service. It was Ali's first visit back home since she left for Columbia. She didn't even return for the high holidays. My parents hadn't mentioned that she was coming. Likely she didn't tell them. Just showed up. I was glad she remembered.

"You ought to get some posters in here," Ali wandered aimlessly around my room, picking stuff up, putting stuff back down. Her mind appeared to be wandering too. A lot.

"Posters?" I said.

"Anything. Dylan. Hendrix. Mao."

"Mao?" I reached for a t-shirt on my floor and slipped it on and then stuffed *The Crying of Lot 49* under my mattress so Ali wouldn't quiz me about it. It was her copy that I had borrowed from her shelves and even though I hardly understood anything I was reading, it was the best damn thing I'd ever read.

"Not Che," Ali said. "Jim Morrison."

"Why not Che?" I asked. "How about Seaver?"

"You're funny," she said. "You were always funny."

I wasn't trying to be funny. I wasn't. I didn't even know what was funny.

"What is that crap you're listening to, Zach?" She sat next to me.

Her brown hair, woven into a braid, reached all the way to my mattress and at that moment I noticed she was pretty. Jonah, my neighbor and my best friend since always, had gotten this giant crush on her, which he insisted on telling me about it in great detail, no matter how many times I told him that I preferred he keep his creepy thoughts about my sister to himself.

"You have got to change the station."

"Change it to what?" I asked.

"Zach," she said abruptly.

I waited for her to continue, but she didn't say a thing. It was like Ali had a point that she kept losing.

"Zach," she said again. This time she looked at me. "You're becoming a man tomorrow. You may as well grow up."

"Okay." I was not following what she was talking about. At all. And then she leaned across me and flipped the white dial on my brown plastic transistor radio from AM to FM. "What does the radio have to do with my Bar Mitzvah?" I asked as she adjusted the dial.

"Stop talking, Zach. Just listen." Her voice trailed off. "Just listen," she repeated as she found a station. The DJ, Paul Jacobs, was talking calmly. He read from a list of meetings and gatherings and happenings around New York. He mentioned places I'd never been to and causes I'd never heard of. Then Jacobs put on a record and dropped the needle on Dylan. My mind exploded as it tried to wrap itself around ideas being used as maps. Each line cried out with consequence and I raced to try and keep up with every word. Lies and jealousy and mutiny and equality. Dylan spoke those words like they were wedding vows and with greater understanding than I could gather.

When the song ended, I was feeling much younger than before Ali walked into my room. Was Dylan right? Was my Bar Mitzvah simply a trick to get me to think I had a tribe to protect? The ritual had been set in motion centuries earlier, and the next morning I would step up to the bema and recite a prescribed sequence of words from ancient texts I had memorized for the occasion. In response, I would be granted privileges and assigned responsibilities of an adult male member of the tribe. Had I been deceived into picking sides, into taking a false stance? Were there sides?

I leaned back exhausted as Paul Jacobs calmly introduced a Phil Ochs tune. I had never heard of Phil Ochs. There was so much more happening here with so much less noise than the AM station Ali had muted. I was wondering how I did not know that this other world had been inside my radio all along.

"You weren't ready before," Ali told me.

"Ready for what?"

"You're still in SP this year, right?"

"Sure." Jonah and I were both in it. It was in our second year, and Ali had also tested high enough in sixth grade to be placed in a Special Program that let you do the three years of Junior High, seventh, eighth, and ninth grade, in just two years. It was like a get out of adolescence jail free pass. Ali was four years ahead of me. Our school had so many students that teachers didn't bother trying to remember us all. I never had to deal much with them calling me Ali's little brother or hearing about how smart she was and all. I mean, I liked that she was smart, real smart, it's just that who needs to be compared all the time. Anyway, I knew that Ali knew about SP.

"It's high school next year? Tenth grade?"

"Yeah," I said.

Ali stood and went to my bookshelf. She put on my Brooklyn Dodgers hat. Then she picked up my Johnny Podres baseball and rolled it around her hand.

"You can have the hat," I said. "I'm a Mets fan."

Because my father couldn't, Ali used to play catch with me when I was little. She had a good arm. And, she was a lefty. But she never played sports.

"You hang on to it," she said. "It's not about the Dodgers. It's about you. It's part of your story. Besides, I bet it finally fits you." Ali replaced the ball next to the framed picture of the Dodgers celebrating Brooklyn's only championship. She slipped the hat on my head. "Leave the hat on. Uncle Herb will be glad to see you wearing it."

She was right. "He's going to tell the story," I said.

"He'll tell it whether you wear the hat or not," she laughed. "Come on," she said. "They were here when I arrived. They wanted me to get you. Let's go eat."

I followed Ali down the stairs.

"You're just in time," our mom said when we entered the dining room. "We're ready to eat."

While my mom and her sister served everyone gefilte fish my Uncle Herb wished me a happy birthday.

"I was there, you know?" he said.

"There?" Ali laughed.

"Where?" I laughed as well.

"Don't encourage him," our dad said.

"I was also there when you were born, Alison," Uncle Herb said to Ali. "But today is Zach's birthday." He turned to me. "I was there when the doctor pulled you out. I was there when the doctor said you were Brooklyn's lucky charm." Uncle Herb retold the whole story of his version of my birth, something he did every year on my birthday. "The doctor brought a TV into the delivery room so he could watch the game."

"He wanted me to keep my legs crossed," my mom said. "He didn't want to miss the final innings of Game 7 of the 1955 World Series."

"That's when we thought we heard your mom scream," Uncle Herb said, "and I brought your dad in to see what was going on."

"Only it wasn't me screaming. The Dodgers made a good play, and everyone in the room screamed."

"The doctor invited us to stay, and I saw the Dodgers win the World Series, and I saw you being born."

"Like being at a doubleheader," I said. I'd been working on that line all week, but I got no response. I'd heard this story so many times that it was like I was there. Which I was. Sort of.

"And then he gave you his signed Johnny Podres ball and told your parents to put it in your left hand," my uncle said.

"And his hat," my mother said.

"He had the nurse write that down for us," my dad said. "Like some medical order."

"I had a few other things on my mind," my mother added.

"But then your parents took you out of Brooklyn," Uncle Herb said. He and Aunt Sadie still lived in Brooklyn and they didn't have any kids. "They broke their promise to the Doctor. And then the Dodgers left town."

"Surely you don't think it's our fault that the Dodgers left Brooklyn?" my father said.

"I didn't say it was your fault."

"Good," my father said.

"I said I was blaming you," Uncle Herb said.

"That's much better," my father said. "But, as I recall, the Dodgers left Brooklyn before we did."

"You take the fun out of a good story," my uncle responded.

• • •

The thing is, every adult in my neighborhood claimed that they either came from another country or Brooklyn. Most swore that they celebrated in the streets that October night in 1955 when the Dodgers beat the Yankees and became World Champions. Forget about it, you'd be hard-pressed to find anyone who ever attended a game at Ebbets Field, or knew how to read a box score, let alone understood the infield fly rule. And it didn't matter that not one of them had been there in 1947 to watch Jackie Robinson hop over the foul line into fair territory and take his place on the field where he smothered ground balls and changed baseball and America forever. What mattered was that the Dodgers were loud, hard working, and totally unsophisticated. They were Brooklyn. And when the Dodgers beat the Yankees on the day I was born, they gave every immigrant proof that in America, the bums did have a chance of coming out on top. The home of the free was truly a land of possibility. But then those same wonderful bums packed up and left without warning. Loaded up the caravan and escaped west, trading air pollution for smog, Coney Island for Malibu, Broadway for Hollywood, and hot dogs for…for who the hell knows what?

Though both my parents spoke several languages, neither spoke baseball. The game was an enigma for those raised on soccer. And they had little interest in learning. After all, the nuances of navigating their new American life, their third country to call home, their third nationality to embrace, their third planting of roots, left little time to decode the idiosyncrasies of baseball.

Until Sandy Koufax.

Sandy made them notice. Sandy gave them a character in the game. Sandy was a left-handed Jew who threw a baseball like no other lefty ever had. Sandy turned the game into a drama they could follow. So in 1963, when this soft-spoken, Brooklyn-born, Jewish-raised, marginally observant Sandy came back to New York with the Los Angeles Dodgers to face the hated Yankees in the World Series, his story gained traction. When he beat the Yankees in Game 1 while striking out a record fifteen batters, and then just a few days later won Game 4 to lead the Dodgers to a World Series sweep, he became a hero. My uncle said he had the left arm of god. But I'm sure he read that in a newspaper.

None of those heroics came close to Sandy's performance the following year when he was scheduled to pitch the first game of the

World Series. That game was to be played on Yom Kippur, a solemn day of fasting and the most visible of Jewish holidays. Sandy announced that he was not going to pitch out of respect for Yom Kippur. What Sandy Koufax was not going to do became the story, and it didn't matter that he wasn't religious or observant, or that we weren't either. Sandy showed it was possible to be Jewish and American.

The following summer, Koufax was scheduled to pitch against the Mets, and my parents surprised me with tickets. It was their first and only baseball game. I wore Dr. Steel's Brooklyn hat, but that didn't stop the Mets from beating Sandy that day. I knew that's the way baseball worked, but I was worried that my parents would be disappointed in Sandy.

"Do not judge the outcome," my father said. "It is a rare moment in life when we can control results. But, we can always control our effort. By that measure," he added, "Sandy's day was a success."

As we made our way out of Shea that evening, my father bought me a Mets hat. "It's time to retire your Brooklyn hat," he said. "It's time you root for the home team."

• • •

"I have a question," Ali interrupted, "why do we celebrate a Bar Mitzvah at the age of thirteen?"

"No politics tonight, Ali," my father said.

"It's not politics, Dad. It's Judaism," Ali said.

I was pretty sure Ali knew that every discussion she started about religion turned into an argument about politics. I'm pretty sure my dad knew she wasn't going to stop.

"Nobody has a guess?" Ali went on. "What about you Zach? You're the Bar Mitzvah boy, right?"

"I am," I laughed, nervously.

"You're going to do great tomorrow, kid," Uncle Herb said.

"Didn't they teach you this?" Ali went on.

They did not, I assured her. The question never came up. But it was a good question, I told her. And, I thought to myself, it seemed like the kind of useful information the Rabbi might have passed along.

"Leave the kid alone," our Grandpa Isaac said to Ali. "He has enough to worry about."

Wait. Why did he say that? Was there something to worry about?

"Leah, your potato pancakes are out of this world," Aunt Sadie told her sister. "So light."

I stuffed another pancake in my mouth.

"The part we left out, Zach," my father said, "is that you don't technically have to do anything to become a Bar Mitzvah."

"I don't?" I said.

"There's no ritual requirement."

"I'm not following," I said. "Didn't I just study for nine months?"

"You just have to turn thirteen," my father said.

"Why all the fuss?"

"Because Jews are Jews simply because of what we read together. Jews are connected by the texts we read. By books we share. And because learning the fundamentals seemed like a good idea to someone a long time ago, and then a few others followed and it became a tradition. And Jews, well, you know, we're big fans of tradition."

I liked traditions. Spring Training. Opening day. Cartoons on Saturday morning. The World Series. "Just to be clear. You're telling me that all the studying I've been doing is not required?"

"Not required," my father said.

"Okay. This is information I could have used earlier."

"What would it have changed?" my father said.

He was right. Required or not, a god or not, I was going to follow through with my Bar Mitzvah. It was part of a contract I had apparently agreed to before I was born. It was non-negotiable, the same way I apparently agreed to let a stranger snip off my foreskin on my eighth day experiencing sunlight. So, I practiced. And I studied. And I learned and memorized and rehearsed and didn't question anything about my role in the Saturday morning ceremony that would add me to the list of adult male members of the tribe of Aaron, a tribe that honored a god who allowed the Holocaust, a god who looked away as my father got polio and became confined to a wheelchair. The Tribe had survived for thousands of years and countless attempts to get rid of it. Who was I to mess with a streak?

"That's all true," Ali said to our dad. "But the question before us is, why does the Bar Mitzvah take place at thirteen. And why do girls get Bat Mitzvah at twelve."

"We mature quicker than boys, dear" Aunt Sadie added.

"We certainly do," Ali said, looking quite satisfied.

Everybody seemed to relax, happy that Ali had made her point without any casualties, and now we could enjoy our feast.

"It's all about physical maturity." Ali wasn't done. "It's about making babies."

That relaxed state evaporated in an instant. I started a body count. This was kind of funny.

"Babies?" Aunt Sadie repeated her niece's words. Uncle Herb and Aunt Sadie were never able to have children.

"Boys can have babies at thirteen. Girls, twelve." Ali paused to make sure everyone was paying attention. She was working her audience. "In the old days, you became a man when you could be fruitful and multiply."

"I can multiply and divide," I said. Everyone laughed, except Ali. Maybe she forgot that I was in honors math.

"Begot and begat," Ali continued.

"Forgot and forget," my father responded. "Ali, enough."

"Becoming a man is about being able to make more Jews," Ali said. "About being able to procreate."

"It's important to make more Jewish babies," my father said. "We have some catching up to do."

"They can't make babies alone," my mother said.

"Exactly," Ali said.

I think my mother was imagining the grandchildren Ali was supposed to get around to giving her.

"You must realize," our Grandpa Isaac said to Ali, "that these laws and customs and rituals and traditions are very old. They were created by a people who rode around on camels and didn't have indoor plumbing. Back then, people grew up quicker. They died young. All labor was manual. Making babies was necessary for survival."

"Okay," I said. "I don't have to make a baby? That's a relief." I got another laugh. And the night was still young.

"I'm with you there, little brother," Ali said. "I have no intention of ever having a kid."

The thing is, this time, I was trying to be funny. This time, I did think we were joking. Instead, I walked right into something.

"What's this about?" Grandpa Isaac asked. He put down his fork and leaned heavily on the table, giving his eldest grandchild all of his attention.

"The world's too screwed up, Grandpa," Ali said. "There's too many people in it already, and disaster's much too certain for me to bring a new life into it. That would be irresponsible."

"So," our father said, "your mother and I are irresponsible for bringing you and Zach into the world?"

"No," Ali said. "That was your choice and this is mine."

"Being responsible and being able to control everything is not the same, Ali." Grandpa Isaac picked up his fork and continued eating.

"I can't stop my kid from being dragged away by death squads in the middle of the night, can't promise them that the ovens have been turned off forever, that the gas chambers have been razed. Can't guarantee that they won't starve or get cancer or be vaporized in a nuclear blast. I couldn't look my kid in the eye and tell him that I could protect them. For that, they would need a god and I could not assure him that any exists. Can you?"

God's existence seemed like a bigger reason for my Bar Mitzvah. The only thing I knew was that I could no more prove there was not a god than someone could prove there was one. I was sure that my doubt was as strong as their belief.

"Life does not come with guarantees," my father said, shifting in his wheelchair.

"That's my point,"Ali said.

My father may have been talking about his polio, though he rarely did. And I wasn't about to ask because there was also the part of his life that had endured devastating personal and communal hardships during the middle third of the 20th century. There was an unspoken agreement among my parents and their parents and their friends, that, having survived the Holocaust, when so many did not, they had an obligation to procreate a new generation of Jews who would prove that Hitler had not been successful.

Faith be damned. Degree of Jewish observance, not significant.

Sure, no one specifically told me that I was a replacement for those children exterminated in the Shoah, but I knew.

That same agreement was why I also knew that I was a Jew even if I didn't want to be Jewish. For that, I had my Grandfather Isaac to thank. He said that even without a god, even without faith, even without observance, I was a Jew. I might choose to ignore, forget, hide that I was a Jew, but the world would still remind me. I could change my name, marry a non-Jew, convert, get plastic surgery to replace the lost foreskin, but when they started looking for Jews, he said, and in time they will, they'd find me. That, I assured him, was a comforting thought.

"You're young still," our mom said. "You'll change your mind."

"Who wants more brisket?" my Aunt asked.

"No. I won't," Ali said. "Not about this. "I'm certain about this."

"We'll see," our father said. "Life has a way of altering our best plans."

"Do you get pleasure from seeing me give up on my ideals?" Ali said.

"How does this qualify as an ideal?" Grandpa Isaac asked.

"Right now I'd get great pleasure from seeing you eat some of your Aunt's brisket," our father said.

"Sure, I'll have more brisket," Ali said. "But this plan won't be altered."

Ali took some brisket, and I put some more on my plate. It was more amazing than usual, and it was usually very good.

"Ali," Grandpa Isaac said, "I'm wondering why you're bringing this up today. Why do you have to decide now?"

"I already decided."

"What does that mean?" our father said loudly.

"I can't have children," Ali said. We waited for her to continue. "I had my tubes tied three weeks ago."

I knew enough to know that this was serious. The sisters gasped. Silverware dropped. My mother grabbed my father's hand. Uncle Herb stood up. Aunt Sadie covered her mouth.

"Dad," my mom said, "take Zach outside while I get dessert ready."

I hadn't even finished my brisket. I grabbed a couple of rolls on my way out.

• • •

Out on the street, the pumpkin sun hung in the sky like it was never going to set. This was a time of day that I pictured children in Kansas or Nebraska helping bring the animals in for the night. The air was so still, every noise seemed muffled. The sounds of television mumbled their way across the neighborhood while sprinklers rhythmically whipped water over small patches of grass.

Grandpa Isaac sat down on the front stoop and lit a cigarette.

"Is it true about the babies?" I asked. I knew I could have kids. I knew about sex and all that stuff, and was almost looking forward to it, but I hoped that there was more to becoming a Bar Mitzvah. The Rabbi never mentioned babies. I would have remembered babies.

"You know Zach," Grandpa Isaac said, exhaling a perfect smoke ring, "we choose what things mean. People do. For me, a Bar Mitzvah is not about babies, it's about stories. Remembering, retelling, and passing on stories. It's about weaving your story into the community. Tomorrow you will read a story in synagogue. People who are present will add your story to theirs. The story grows. The story goes on."

"Not all stories are good stories, Grandpa. Especially our stories, Jewish stories. Our history is like a series of apocalyptic novels that never seems to end."

"Those are stories we all need to remember, but not relive. If we retell them, and retell them, and retell them, then just maybe we will have a chance to not repeat them. To not relive them."

"Like Passover."

Behind us, Ali pushed open the screen door and came out. She sat on the other side of Grandpa, pulled out one of his cigarettes and used his lighter. "It's a beautiful night, Grandpa," she said, exhaling a large white cloud.

"And yet you don't think it's a beautiful world?"

"It can be a beautiful world. I'm quite capable of deluding myself about that. But, I can only find beauty in the night sky because everything looks better from a distance. But close up. Close up they killed Robert Kennedy. They murdered Martin Luther King. Malcolm X, too. Newark is burning. Detroit, Watts, Paris. On fire. Chicago looks like Montgomery. Johnson abandoned his War on Poverty. He sold out his dream of a Great Society to pay for destroying Vietnam and sending American boys to die in the jungle and now we're going to get Nixon as a reward."

Grandpa Isaac nodded at the sky. "Do you think there's life out there?"

"I'd bet on it," Ali said. "I don't see how there couldn't be. I just hope they're doing better than we are because we're destroying ourselves."

"Plus, who could prove you wrong?" I said.

Both of them looked at me.

"If you bet on it, no one could prove you wrong?" I repeated.

"You are getting very funny," Ali said. "Isn't he, Grandpa?"

"The best way to protect the world from harming itself," Grandpa Isaac said to Ali, "is to change it."

"What if the change is what destroys it?" Ali said.

"It makes me glad that you can imagine other life in the universe," our grandfather said. "As long as you can imagine, then life has hope. And we require hope to live. And we require imagination to change. Hope and imagination. Unless we can imagine a better world, we will remain stuck with this one."

"I can imagine Auschwitz," Ali said. "I can imagine Zachary going to Vietnam."

I did not like her imagining me going to Vietnam. I was sure that if I went, it would not end well. "They say that there are more stars in the sky than grains of sand on Earth." I tried to change the topic.

The stars were lighting up the autumn sky, joining the moon that had been visible for hours. I tried to trace the Big Dipper as I peered into the old darkness of ancient space. I was looking at the past. Much of what I saw no longer existed.

"Imagining Auschwitz is easy," Grandpa Isaac said. "It takes almost no imagination for that. You need to imagine a world without

Auschwitz. That's the challenge. That's what I'm counting on you for. We all are."

"Not my parents."

"Especially your parents. They just don't know how to tell you. And if they did, I'm not sure you would be able to hear it." He said and released a smoke ring. "You know the one thing that's even more painful than discovering that your parents are human?"

"What?" Ali said.

"Admitting that you are."

Ali leaned over and kissed Grandpa Isaac on the cheek. She slid closer to him, locked elbows, and rested her head on his shoulder.

"If people don't have kids, then won't life on Earth end?" I asked Ali under the protective glance of our grandfather.

"Would that be so bad?" she said, turning her head to blow smoke out of her mouth. "Anyway, little brother, there's plenty of other people making babies."

I sat up straight. Hadn't she noticed that I was already taller than her?

"You know, Zach," Grandpa Isaac told me, "I'm ambivalent about god. But what I know is that Judaism is less about believing and more about doing. The more Jewish things I do, the more Judaism comes alive to me. The Talmud teaches that it's not necessary for each person to complete a whole task, it's only important that they do their part."

"And my part," Ali said, "is not having kids."

"That may be," Grandpa Isaac said to Ali. "But of this I am certain. That is not your only part. You have much more to do."

"How will I know what my part is?" I asked.

"No one can tell you, but finding out is what makes life interesting," Isaac said. He rubbed out his cigarette against the concrete step. "Zach, do you remember the first time I introduced you to Mr. Alberts in 3G and I told you he was blind?"

"Not really," I said.

"I guess you were only four years old. Anyway, I asked you if you knew what blind was and you answered, 'No, it's when you can't see.'"

Ali and I laughed.

"You knew the right words, but you couldn't imagine blind. You weren't ready. It's the same thing now. You're not ready to know your part. But that doesn't mean you can't start searching." He stood. "In the meantime, I'm ready for dessert. They've had enough time to say whatever they needed to say and move on."

"We're going to take a walk, Grandpa," Ali said.

"We are?" I asked.

"I'll let them know."

"I guess I ruined your dinner," Ali turned to me. We were still on the stoop.

"That's okay," I answered. I think she meant it. "I wasn't hungry."

"Again, funny."

"I'm looking forward to who you become, Zach," she said. "But for now, I have something for your Bar Mitzvah."

"Thanks," I said. "You didn't have to."

"I mean, I'm going to give it to you now."

"But I didn't do anything yet."

"Let's take a walk."

"Okay."

Ali wanted to go somewhere private. I led us to the Little League fields. We turned onto Short Street and then down Hernia Hill.

As Ali held on to my arm, we descended the extremely steep and immensely dangerous Hernia Hill. At the bottom, we crossed both sets of tracks and walked onto the last of the four baseball fields. Ali sat on the bench in the third-base dugout and pulled a pack of cigarettes from her pocket. She removed a crumpled cigarette and offered it to me.

"I don't smoke," I said.

"Good," Ali said. "And don't start. But this is a joint." When I didn't respond, she added, "Pot. You know, marijuana, not a cigarette."

"Okay." That was all I could come up with.

"You've never tried any?"

"*I'm thirteen.*" I didn't mean to say it that way.

"I'm going to light it and pass it to you. When you take it, inhale slowly, and then hold your breath as long as you can. Okay?" Ali instructed me. "But don't inhale too deep at first."

"Cool." I was pretty sure I thought it was cool. I was ready for cool. I was. I just needed help picking what new stuff was cool and what was not. That meant figuring out which adults to follow and which not. Ali was my sister and she was right about the radio. Maybe she was also right about pot.

Ali lit a match and I watched as she inhaled. The smoke had a kind of skunk smell to it, but not in a bad way.

"Here," Ali said through her held breath.

I took the joint. Inhale and hold it, I said to myself. Inhale and hold it. I looked at the reefer between my fingers one more time and wondered what my life was going to be like after I inhaled. Was I more scared of trying or not trying new things?

"Don't waste it," Ali said through her used up smoke. "Zach, you have to trust new stuff even if it scares the shit out of you. Especially if it scares the shit out of you. It's the only thing that can save you."

"What do I need saving from?"

"From sleepwalking through life."

"Am I sleepwalking?"

"Not yet. But it's what happens to adults," Ali said.

"And this will help?"

"No more talking."

I put the tip between my lips and sucked air. The smoke expanded and filled my lungs until they could hold no more and I coughed hard, unable to hold the smoke. I held the joint out for Ali as I buckled over, sucking in fresh air.

"Tiny breath," Ali said, passing the joint back to me.

This time I barely inhaled. I felt the smoke fill my lungs again, but I did not cough. I held my breath. It was like learning to swim. Finally, I released the warm stream of smoke from my lungs. Ali and I finished two joints with determination and not much talking. Something was happening and I did not know what it was.

"That was fun," Ali said.

"Are we criminals?"

"Outlaws."

"Like cowboys?"

"Like revolutionaries," Ali said.

"What revolution are we part of?" I asked.

"The revolution that is happening all around us," she said.

"Where?"

"All you have to do is look."

"In my room you said all I had to do was listen," I said.

"Look and listen."

"To what?" I said.

"Everything," she said. "Change is everywhere. Just look all around you."

"Is change always good?"

"It's always inevitable."

"How will I know when I'm high?" I asked.

"Sometimes it takes longer the first time you smoke, but you'll know when you're high."

"Are you high?"

"I was high when I got home, little brother. It's the only way for me to tolerate being home," she said. "Relax for a while. Let's smoke another joint and then we'll walk back home for your birthday cake ritual."

"What if I'm high and don't know it and no one tells me that I'm high?"

"No one will have to tell you," Ali assured me.

"Okay." I believed her.

We smoked another joint and started walking back.

"You know how they say it's always calm just before the storm?" I said as we climbed up Hernia Hill.

"Who?"

"I don't know. People."

"Sure."

"It's not true. It's never calm before the storm."

"Okay," Ali said, laughing.

"I'll tell you another thing."

"Please."

"It's not always darkest before the dawn. I stayed up all night and that's not true either." I was feeling bold. "Are you not going to have kids?" I asked.

"I'm not," Ali said, "but let's not talk…"

"You're very brave," I blurted.

"I think it's braver to have kids."

"You're wrong. Going along with what everyone else is doing is never brave. Like I think it's easier to go to Vietnam than not."

"You know why nothing changes," Ali said.

"No," I said. "Do you?"

"Anyone who can change things won't because they don't want to displease their parents or embarrass their kids."

"That's not bad," I started laughing. "But it's wrong."

"Wrong?"

"Incorrect, mistaken, inaccurate, not right."

"Four words that mean wrong." Ali was laughing. "And you have a better theory?"

"Yes. Not just better, right."

"Let's hear it."

"Greed."

"Greed?"

"Greed makes people do bad things. It makes people bitter, makes them steal what is not theirs, and often what they do not need. Steal stuff, steal money, steal freedom. Lying is stealing the truth. Killing is stealing a life."

Ali put her hand on my shoulder and stopped me. I turned to look at her and she put her other hand on my other shoulder.

"Congratulations, Zach," Ali said to me. "You are officially stoned." She didn't say anything else for a while, she just stared at me as if looking for something.

Maybe I was supposed to say something?

"Yes, you are now a man," she finally said. "Be careful how you use it." She removed her hands from my shoulders and started walking.

"Wait," I said, catching up to her. "What does that even mean?"

"You'll figure that out soon enough."

"I'd figure it out quicker if you just told me," I said.

When we could see our house, Ali smiled, "One last thing."

"What?" I said.

"When we get back there will be cake and dessert. You're going to have the urge to eat a lot."

"Okay," I said.

"Don't fight it."

The adults were all smiles seeing us together. They didn't ask where we had been. We were smiling too. I think my parents were happy Ali wanted to hang out with me. I also think they were a little scared of her and were willing to sacrifice me.

My mother brought out my birthday cake and other treats. I blew out the candles without making a wish.

Later, after our parents went to bed, and Ali went out to meet some friends, I went upstairs to my room and turned on the radio. Paul Jacobs had left, and a woman was on the air. Her name was Jenny and she called herself the Night Owl. She read poetry between songs. I didn't know I loved poetry. I wanted Jenny to talk forever. I drifted off to sleep with the sounds of Jim Morrison singing about the end seeping into my brain.

• • •

The next morning I overslept, leaving no time to be nervous. In temple, I was called to the bema. And there, like so many other thirteen year old males in synagogues all around New York, I chanted the weekly portion of the Haftorah and received the Rabbi's blessing. That was that. I was a man. And wasn't it a man's world? What was the effect of all those ancient words being chanted together? Of so many boys becoming men? I hoped something. I feared nothing.

During his speech to the congregation, the Rabbi said that god's answers were incomprehensible to us because we were only human and incapable of understanding the complexity of his answers. I don't know what he said next because that sentence froze my brain. It would have caused an aneurysm had I not noticed Amy Black sitting in the third row. Ali was right about girls maturing before boys, and Amy was maturing before the other girls. My view of her maturity from up on the bema was excellent. I wondered if the Rabbi was seeing the same unbuttoned shirt. I wondered if the Rabbi always had this excellent view.

Later that afternoon, when the last guest left our house, Ali helped me open and log my presents so I could write thank you cards at a later date. Our parents didn't pay us any mind as they cleaned up around us. When an envelope had cash, Ali smiled and removed a bill or two which she slipped into an envelope. When we were done, she handed me the envelope before she gathered the pile of bonds and checks and cash which she handed to my mother who promised to take me to open a bank account in both our names.

After Ali headed back to Columbia, and after the final in a long series of extended hugs from my mother, I went up to my room where I counted the money Ali separated and set aside for me. I found a safe place for the cash and reached under my mattress for my book. I found a Marlboro box on which Ali had written the word Outlaws. Inside were a lot of joints. I removed one, replaced the box, grabbed my coat, and climbed through my bedroom window onto my roof.

I lit Ali's joint and inhaled confidence. All sorts of people claimed that they spoke directly to god. Some announced that they alone were delivering messages straight from god. Liars and frauds were the nicest labels I had for them. When I read those five books of the Torah it became clear that god went silent toward the end. Sure, god spoke the world into existence, but then seemed to lack the attention span to keep the conversation going. Yes, Adam and Eve were on a first name basis, but they didn't know any better. And god talked to Noah and then Abraham, but that was like a sentence here or there, hardly a discussion. He went silent while the tribe was stuck in Egypt until Moses brought him out of retirement. Moses was the last human who god had any real conversation with. Maybe it was because Moses talked back, even disagreed. But as each of those five books of Moses rolled along, fewer and fewer people were granted a one-on-one conversation. If you ask me, after Moses, god either lost control or lost interest or lost patience with people and moved on. If you ask me, I think god just didn't have much to say to us.

The Rabbi said we learned by asking questions. Sure, you need to ask the right question to get a useful answer. But the key there was getting an answer that made sense. How do you hit a curveball? How do you get a girl to notice you? I learned a lot from answers. What kind of god would expect people to know what to do when they couldn't understand the instructions? My money was on god not understanding our questions, or that he stopped listening. That would explain the mess we were in.

Like that time I took the wrong bus to the museum. Imagine if I asked the driver if I was on the wrong bus and I didn't understand her answer. What was I supposed to do, keep asking questions? Is this a bus? What is a bus? Are any buses right? Is it my destiny to find the right bus? By that time I would have been in the Bronx and forever lost.

The roof was my fortress of solitude. I went there to relive my day and rearrange events in my favor. I redirected fly balls into my glove, made the winning basket, held a wheelie just that much longer, and said the right things at the right time to the cool kids and the girls. Satisfied with the new outcomes, I planned my next day's strategies with renewed hope and promise.

Up on my roof, I was Kal-El, Superman's Hebrew name. The voice of god. Those wimpy Jewish boys from Cleveland who created Superman, Jerry Siegel and Joe Shuster, hurtled their baby Superman through space in a basket like baby Moses. Maybe they were also looking around them for an adult to follow, to save the people of Earth from themselves, and when they came up empty they invented Superman. Ali had said that she hoped there was other life out there in the universe. I hoped that included Superman. We needed Superman. But did we deserve him?

The thing that made Supe special to me was that he led a solitary, selfless, lonely existence because it was the only way to protect the people he cared about. He was Superman and he could do or take whatever he wanted. But he never chose to turn his back on people, despite there being nothing in it for him. That was the cost of doing the right thing. There was always a price to be paid for greatness, my grandfather used to tell me. Up on my roof, I tried to summon my Kal-

El. I needed my Clark Kent to reveal his Superman.

When the joint became too small to grip, I rubbed out the ash on the shingles and moved higher up on the roof and peaked out over the ridge at the street below. Tall oaks and maples, trees that had been in the neighborhood longer than my family, lined the block in front of the rows and rows of small, single family, brick houses. I could see all the important places in my neighborhood from my roof.

Two houses to the right, on the opposite side of the street, was Jonah's house. We had lived across the street from each other our whole lives.

There weren't any lights on in his house. Two blocks past Jonah's house was the elementary schoolyard with its asphalt clearing. The prairie fenced in. We knew every hole in the fence, every hop on the stickball court, every bump on the shuffleboard, where the afternoon sun made the centerfielder lose a fly ball, and exactly when each of the three ice cream trucks stopped by. It was where Jonah and I had first ventured out together to meet the challenges of our day. Together, we had left the safety of that neighborhood haven for new and bigger schoolyards.

Leaving places and people, moving on, seemed inevitable.

I slid down the shingles and back into my room and into my bed where I turned on the radio. Jenny, my Night Owl, was still on the air. She read a poem by Allen Ginsburg. I wanted her to just keep reading to me. I wanted the best minds of my generation to solve the war. And everything else. But at that moment, all I wanted was to keep listening to her voice.

PIECE OF MY HEART

I first met Tony in gym class, at the beginning of the school year, soon after my Bar Mitzvah. Actually, I was trying very hard to avoid meeting him. In gym class or anywhere else. I recognized him from around the school. He was already shaving, and rumor had it that he had punched a teacher and already had his learner's permit. Only the permit was true. Tony was old enough to be in Jonah's sister Wendy's grade. That day in the gym, we were put on the same three-on-three, round-robin basketball team. While we were waiting for our game I tried to avoid eye contact, or any contact. Then Tony asked me if I was in the two year SP.

I mumbled yes.

"I'm in the four-year program, myself," Tony said.

I tried to not laugh, but I did.

"But they'll let me out this year. I know they will."

"Cool." I had no idea why he was talking to me.

"That fourth year is like having a free pass. I am aware that teachers wouldn't want me back in their class a third time and will pass me no matter what I do or don't do."

Tony kept talking. I was glad because it meant I didn't have to. I was worried that I'd say the wrong thing and make him mad.

"Let me run something by you," Tony said as our game started. "Do you think telling a teacher that *my soul was being crushed by the magnitude of the historical injustice in the world,* is a good excuse for my history homework being late?"

"Works for me." I finally laughed.

"See, it's funny because it's true."

Tony did not like playing sports. He was opposed to sweating. But that's not what made him different. I had never met anyone who talked like Tony. He was a human radio. And completely convincing no matter what he was saying. Even when I knew he was bullshitting, I believed him. He and Jonah and I became fast friends.

The thing that had quickly become clear to me about Tony was that teachers didn't need to pass him just to get rid of him. If they couldn't figure out that he was, by every other measure besides school, incredibly smart then they were in the wrong profession.

I was with him that night when he met Mel. A McDonald's had opened on Continental Avenue, and none of us had ever been to one, and Tony wanted to check it out. As we entered the brightly lit space Tony nodded toward this cute girl at the counter. I followed him to her line. Her name tag said Mel. When we got to the counter she smiled and asked, "How can I help you?"

I waited for Tony to order. He just stood there, looking at Mel and shaking his head slowly. "I appreciate your concern," he said and then went into a litany of issues and challenges he needed help with. He let Mel know she was free to pick any one of them and start there. "Many have tried to help," he said. "but none have yet succeeded. Still," he added, leaning in toward Mel, "I have a good feeling about you. I have high hopes for you. I am in fact completely confident that you can help me."

Mel looked around and then leaned forward. Tony leaned in even closer as she whispered. "It's not that I don't think your problems are serious," she said. "They're totally serious. I mean you have some completely fucked up issues you should deal with. But here's the thing.

They're just not very interesting. So, either order some food or go kill yourself."

Tony stood up and grinned. "Did you hear her?" he smiled at me. "That was genius." He turned back toward her. "Mel," he said. "I'm Tony and I'm in love." And then he ordered us food. A lot of food. I don't know if he wanted to try everything they had to offer, if he wanted to still be eating when Mel's shift ended, or if he thought Mel worked on commission.

Tony and Mel had been dating ever since.

II

1969

SUMMER IN THE CITY

Instead of starting each morning scanning box scores and calculating when the Mets would be eliminated from the playoffs, I had begun turning the newspaper to the page that listed casualties in Vietnam. You could blame my sister Ali. Or you could give her credit. She had mailed me a small moleskin notebook and pen for my upcoming junior high graduation in which she inscribed – *change is coming – document it.* She also stuck a note inside letting me know she would not be coming home to attend the ceremony. Since the first of June, I had been using that notebook to record a daily count of how many US soldiers had died in Vietnam.

I trusted numbers and hoped they could help me make sense of the war. Thirty-five thousand US soldiers had been killed in Vietnam since the first troops were sent in as advisors. Seven thousand had died since the baseball season's first pitch was thrown out at Shea Stadium. There did not seem to be an end to the dying and the more soldiers Nixon sent to Vietnam, the higher the death toll rose.

I responded the only way that came naturally to me. First I freaked the hell out. And then I freaked Jonah out. Well, maybe less freaked him out, more annoyed him. Okay, maybe he was less than interested when I began reciting the daily death toll on our way to school each day.

"Eleven games, Zach," Jonah said on our walk to school. "How do you not notice an eleven game winning streak? In a row, for god's sake. In a row."

"I know what a streak is," I said.

"Where's your head at?"

"One American soldier is going to die during the time it takes us to walk to school," I said, pulling out my little book.

"Does knowing that make any difference?" Jonah said.

"I'm not sure," I said. I needed answers and no one had any, so I had to pay attention to everything. That's what Ali had told me, and she was the smartest person I knew.

"Then why are you telling me?" he said in frustration.

"Because it's important."

"Did I kill him?" Jonah asked me.

"You most certainly did not," I said.

"Do I know anyone who killed him?"

"I doubt it."

"Did I send him to Vietnam?"

"You did not."

"Do I know anyone who sent him?"

"No."

"Okay," Jonah said. "Put that thing away. We're almost at school."

"Notebooks are allowed at school."

"We're skipping our Junior High Prom after graduation."

"We have a prom?" I asked.

"Yes."

"Okay. I was unaware."

"We have a prom," he repeated.

"How did you find out?"

"They announce it every day. And there are like a hundred posters all over the school."

"And we were going?"

"We were not," Jonah said.

"But now we're skipping it?"

"Yes."

"How do we skip something we weren't going to go to?" I asked. "Is there an announcement involved?"

"We're going to Tony's graduation party."

"Really?"

"It's going to be amazing."

"How did you hear about it?" I asked. "Were there posters for that too?"

"I saw Tony last night at the supermarket," Jonah said.

• • •

When school ended, there was a riot on Christopher Street in the West Village. And it wasn't about the war or race. What happened was that the regular homosexual patrons of the Stonewall Inn, weary of yet another humiliating shakedown by New York City's finest, refused to cooperate on what should have simply been their night out.

Word quickly spread through the Village, to nearby bars, through neighborhood apartments, and over to Washington Square Park, bringing a huge crowd outside the Stonewall. While most came to see what there was to see, others joined the protest and many of those arrested weren't even at the bar when the riot started.

I listened to Paul Jacobs as he interviewed a witness on his radio show. Jacobs said there were reports that the revolt was triggered by a transvestite. The witness said he saw it happen. He said the riot was sparked by a high-heeled boy who smacked a police officer on the head with her pocketbook. That was exactly the kind of trigger that revolutions are ignited by, Paul said. I could hear him smile through the radio. Imagine, he added, seemingly to himself, imagine the possibilities when those who don't usually make any noise unite, when the silent ones and the silenced ones come together with common cause.

Later in the summer, Tony and Jonah and I watched Apollo 11 head for the Moon. The Moon. Like Ken Kesey's bus, they were going farther because further is where humans had always risked going. When we got to the Moon, we stood on its surface, we gathered Moon rocks, we collected Moon dust, and we played Moon golf. And, like on every human exploration on Earth, we planted a flag. And when we departed, we left our garbage behind.

After we came back to Earth we landed at Woodstock. The thing about Woodstock was that it didn't just happen, it mattered. Rock and roll mattered. Hippies mattered. Change mattered. Jimi Hendrix played the national anthem and it mattered because he took it back for us, for every single person in these united spaces. And when the rains came and flooded the grounds that held half a million people, and instead of fire, we had the rainbow sign.

Three days of peace, love, and understanding. Really, who could argue with that? And why would anyone want to?

An anti-war demonstration was planned for Central Park for Labor Day weekend that was expected to dwarf every previous protest, and Jonah decided that we were going. I never minded when Jonah made up my mind. Jonah was cool. I wasn't. I understood cool. I recognized cool. But I couldn't pull off cool. The thing about Jonah was that even though he knew he was cool, and even though he knew that I was not then and would never, ever be cool, he would always have my back.

"It's not Woodstock," Jonah was telling us about the protest in the park. We had met up with Tony and Mel who were hanging out at the schoolyard. Jonah wanted all of us to go together. "But, it's free music. Lots of girls. And plenty of pot. A brilliant combination."

"Outstanding," I said.

"When did you get outstanding?" Jonah asked.

"I thought of it last night. I'm trying to make it work."

“I like it,” Mel said.

“I need something. Especially with starting high school on Tuesday.” I really did need something for tenth grade. I sounded ridiculous when I tried to pull off “groovy” or “far out” or “bummer” or “lay it on me.” I couldn’t make those work. I settled on “outstanding.” I was glad Jonah approved.

“You do,” Tony said. “Seriously, you do.”

“Outstanding,” I said.

“Don’t abuse it,” Tony said.

“Unlikely,” I responded.

“So, it’s settled,” Jonah said. “We’re going to Central Park on Saturday. Just promise me one thing Zach. Promise me you won’t spend the whole time talking about the war.”

“Really?” I said. “You’re abolishing the first amendment?”

“It’s for your own good. When you start your monologue about Vietnam everyone around you wants to kill themselves.”

“They do?” I asked.

“Everyone,” Jonah said.

“Everyone?” I asked.

“Everyone,” Tony agreed.

“And the girls,” Jonah said, “the girls, they just walk away.”

“Do you want the girls to walk away?” Mel asked.

“I do not.”

“Neither do I,” Jonah said. “So, you may not, under any circumstances, talk about the war when we’re at the park,” Jonah said.

“It’s an ANTI-WAR protest,” I protested.

“Exactly. Everyone is already against the war,” Jonah said.

• • •

On Saturday morning, I showered while Crosby, Stills, & Nash sang a new song about wooden ships on my brown plastic radio. I had wired my radio in the bathroom so that whenever I turned on the light, I had music. It was the same radio that Ali had turned from AM to FM the day before my Bar Mitzvah and opened up my world.

The song ended, and Paul Jacobs described his walk to work through Central Park. He often described a Manhattan scene at the beginning of his show. He spoke about summer in New York like he was sitting in a diner talking to a waitress pouring him coffee. Some days, Paul chose to describe a softball game he had passed on Central Park's Great Lawn. He did it in such detail and with such enthusiasm that he could have been talking about, and I could have been listening to, the World Series.

Paul loved baseball as much as music and would talk endlessly about how they were similar, about how clocks stood still at a game or during a song. Some nights he would put together baseball teams made of musicians. Dylan had to pitch of course. He was crafty. You'd never guess what he was going to throw. Paul Simon on second. Hendrix at short. He had great range. Jerry Garcia on first. Probably batting cleanup. Some nights, Jonah and I would draft teams against each other. The possibilities were endless. The combinations intriguing. Why did it make sense that Frank Zappa would make a great pitcher and that Steve Winwood was a centerfielder? Paul said he valued baseball's ability to offer complete moments – the moment a fly ball reached its peak, the moment an infielder stepped toward a ground ball, the moment before the bat made contact. Everything made sense then. Chaos was in check during those moments. Good moments. Like in a Hendrix solo or a Dylan lyric.

Paul Jacobs knew stuff and I was comforted by listening to his show.

I shut the light which shut the radio and went to my room to get dressed. Then I went downstairs, said goodbye to my parents, shut the house door behind me, and went to meet Jonah.

Outside, Jonah and I strolled past the single family brick houses which gradually gave way to duplexes that gave way to small stores and apartment buildings. At the same time, the streets widened until we reached Queens Boulevard where the traffic became steady. We turned left and entered Joe's Candy Shop. That place had been there since forever. They made the best vanilla egg creams. These days Joe's always had a group of hippies sitting with the old men at the counter, a windfall from having Further Records next door. Joe's bacon cheeseburger had become a legendary cure for the munchies. It was so good no one cared that Joe refused to play rock and roll. He only played jazz. John Coltrane, Miles Davis, Charlie Parker. After a while, the record store added a jazz section.

I got us some gum because, well, there might be girls. When we came out Tony and Mel were there.

Tony wanted to get some rolling papers, so we entered Further Records which was also a head shop. Tony asked for two packs of Ziggy's.

"What are you going to use them for?" the guy behind the counter responded.

No one asked us that before.

"You're too young to smoke."

"They're for my dad," Mel said. "He rolls his own cigarettes."

"We don't have to answer that," Tony said. "If something is legal to sell, then it's legal to buy, and it's no one's fucking business what you are going to use it for."

"He's right," someone behind us said. I turned to see this guy sitting on a stool, reading a newspaper, and wearing a Grateful Dead t-shirt. He had a bandana covering the top of his head. "Zander is just screwing with you," he continued without looking up.

Zander laughed. "I was just messing with you." He placed the papers on the counter.

"You can wipe your ass with them and it's no one's fucking

business," the guy behind us added.

"Why would you want to wipe your ass with tiny pieces of rolling paper?" Zander laughed. "You are one sick motherfucker,"

"Are you making an accusation?" the guy laughed.

"More like an assertion," Zander said. "You listen to your friend and to Leo. Even if he is demented. He's a freaking lawyer. Passed the bar and everything."

"You really should use them to roll joints," Zander called out to us as we left the store.

• • •

"They're expecting over a hundred thousand people," Jonah said after we transferred to the F Train.

"Were they expecting us?" I asked.

"You're either very funny," Jonah said to me, "or a moron."

"Why can't I be both?"

"Not easy being you," Mel said.

"So hurtful," I said. "Why do you insist on being so hurtful?"

The train stopped and the four of us climbed the stairs to Fifth Avenue and found ourselves being pulled along by the current of people heading toward the Bandshell. There were so many things to look at, so many people to take notice of, so many images to aspire to. Everyone was trying to make their mark, carve out a niche. I too was trying to be different, like everyone else. I wanted to be John Lennon, but I felt like Ringo.

Mel spotted an empty patch of grass and we claimed it. On one side, these shirtless guys were painting "HELL NO WE WON'T GO" on a large white sheet. On the other side, some girls were painting each other. Tony rolled a joint, lit it, and offered it to the closest girl. As we smoked, one of the girls started to paint a peace sign on Jonah's arm. Girls didn't react to me like they did to Jonah. I used to think it was because he was cool, but that wasn't all of it. He was better looking than me.

"I'm going to find a pretzel," I said, standing. "Anyone want anything?"

"You buying or just looking?" Jonah said.

"What does that mean?" the painting girl asked. Her name was Carla. "Is that like code for acid?"

"No, my man Zach has been on a quest for the perfect pretzel. He thinks he had one when he was eight."

"Seven. And I remember it like it was yesterday," I said. "And I've never found one that good since."

Jonah said. "He's always disappointed."

"What an awful way to live," Carla said, finishing the peace sign on Jonah's arm.

"That's what I tell him," Mel said.

"And yet I remain optimistic that I'll find it."

"You guys are so weird." Carla looked up. "I like weird," she said to Jonah.

"He's like Don Quixote," Jonah said, "without a donkey."

"That's hilarious," Carla laughed. "But Don rode a horse. Sancho rode a donkey."

"My feet are my trusted steed," I said. "I leave you in my quest of the perfect pretzel. It's out there somewhere waiting for me, warming itself, as I speak, on a bed of hot coals. Crusty and salted on the outside and when I twist off a piece, steam will rise from its soft inside and all will be good with the world."

Carla turned to me. "Godspeed on your quest to restore dignity among pretzels."

"You can get me an imperfect pretzel," Jonah said.

"And me as well," Carla laughed.

"Get us all pretzels," Tony said.

"Yes, my lords and my ladies," I said, bowing. I turned to leave and then turned back. “Hey,” I said, “what did the Buddhist say to the hot-dog vendor?” I didn’t wait for a response. “Make me one with everything,” I answered, turned, and left.

“Get me a dog too,” Jonah yelled. “With everything.”

In the crowd, there was something happening, and I wanted to know what it was. I wanted in; to be a part of that something. I stood in the middle of the people and tried to absorb whatever it was. That something in the air. And then I smelled pretzels warming on charcoal. I followed the scent, bought five pretzels, and ran back.

“Where’s my hot dog?” Jonah said. He was smiling at me, still sitting next to Carla.

“Long line.”

I passed out pretzels and Carla introduced me to the rest of our new grassy knoll neighbors. Phil Ochs came on the stage and started singing about the war being over. Carla jumped up and started dancing. She offered her hand to Jonah who took it and followed her closer to the stage. Tony and Mel did the same.

As I lay alone on the grass and listened to songs about universal soldiers, about unions, about Vietnam, I was met with more questions. Did the army have to destroy villages to save them? Were we burning children with napalm? How would I make sense of it all? How would I know who was right if everyone was wrong?

I felt like I was standing on the sidelines.

Then Ochs sang, “We ain't gonna study war no more.” It was like he was trying to will us to stop studying war, and I wanted to know if I had been studying war. What did it mean to study peace? As the crowd sang along, I stood up and joined in. Singing that song in the park together with hundreds of thousands of people made me feel like I was part of something.

I kept hearing that the country needed a revolution, and I believed it. But, I was sure that the revolution would not be one of ideas, of philosophies, of principles. It would be one of bloodshed. Even more, it would end up being one of power. And I did not need a weatherman to know which way the bullets would flow.

• • •

When the music stopped, Jonah found me. "That was cool," he said. Carla was no longer with him as she and her friends had taken some acid and were on their way over to the West Side. He told me that Tony and Mel had to go down to Little Italy to see his grandmother and would catch up with us later.

The crowd began to thin out. We started to do the same when someone climbed onto the Beethoven statue and draped a peace flag over it. The one where they replaced the fifty stars with a peace sign but left the thirteen stripes. It was pretty cool looking, and the crowd cheered him on. But then several guys came running up and pulled him and his flag down to the ground where they began to kick him. I looked for the police I had seen earlier, but they were no longer around.

"Should we help him?" I asked Jonah.

"Those guys are really big," Jonah said. "So, sure."

As we got closer, I noticed the guy getting kicked had a tattoo on his forearm that read *Semper Fidelis*. "He's a vet," I yelled. "He's a Marine," I yelled louder. "Show some respect."

"Respect this," someone behind me yelled.

I turned and that's when I felt a fist hit my chest that caused all the air in my lungs to escape. I buckled over and gasped for air as the fist landed on my cheek. I felt warm blood dripping down my cheek and tasted it at the same moment I landed on the asphalt. Then a boot forced all remaining wind out of me and I couldn't breathe.

Jonah jumped on the guy's back, trying to get him to stop kicking me.

"Do you want to make this your fight?" he asked Jonah.

"What would that involve?" Jonah answered as the guy threw him off.

As I lay there anticipating the next blow, a swarm of police appeared, and the thugs ran off. The police helped me and Jonah up and then they made us put our hands on a tree while they frisked us.

"Do you know that guy?" one officer asked me, pointing to the Vet who remained on the ground.

"No." I was surprised that I was able to stand.

"Why did you get involved? Are you a commie?" he asked.

"He's a vet," I said, "a Marine."

"Are you an NVA sympathizer?" the officer barked at me. "That's what waving that damn flag says to me, punk!"

"It's a peace flag," I said. "And they were kicking him."

"Did you have drugs? Where did you put them?"

"What?" I said. "No."

He started reaching in my pants pockets. Luckily, we had smoked all our pot.

Jonah interrupted the officer searching me and told him I was the one assaulted. The other officer pushed Jonah, pressing him against the trunk of the tree, and searched through his pockets, too. By then, a small crowd had gathered.

"Leave them alone," someone yelled.

"They were the ones getting the crap beat out of them," another yelled. I wondered if he needed to put it that way.

The crowd started hurling insults at the police and then someone hurled a soda bottle in our direction. I think they were aiming at the cops. It missed me and Jonah, but I wasn't sure they were helping as the frisking got rougher.

The officer frisking Jonah got a call on his radio. "Fuck these punks," he said to his partner. "We have to go."

The crowd cheered as the police left. Jonah put his hand on my shoulder. "You okay?"

"Possibly," I said. "You were outstanding."

A woman came over to us. She was a nurse and wanted to take a look at us. Her name was Colleen and she had served in Vietnam with the guys in army jackets who were helping the vet still lying on the ground.

"This guy needs the ER, Colleen," one said. They helped him up.

"Let me make sure these kids are okay," she replied. She checked us out and told us that nothing was broken. She told me that the boot bruised my ribs when it knocked the wind out of me. We didn't need to go to the hospital, but, she added, we'd be sore for a while. Especially me. While wiping my face with a bandana, Colleen told us what we did was very stupid. I wanted her to tell me about Vietnam. When she was done, she repeated that we were very foolish, but that she was proud of us for looking out for a vet. She left us and joined her friends who were on their way to the ER. By then, the crowd had lost interest in us, and we were alone. We started laughing as we limped out of the park.

"What would that involve?" I said as we emerged onto 59th Street. "That was your answer?" It hurt to laugh. "You're nuts," I added. "Those guys were huge."

"I'm an idiot," Jonah said.

• • •

When we reached the horse carriages on Central Park South, someone jumped on my back and covered my eyes. My body was sore, and it was hard to stay standing.

"Hey, little brother," I heard Ali say as she jumped off of me. She hadn't been home since my Bar Mitzvah, choosing to stay in Manhattan with friends after her first year at Columbia. She had told our parents that one of her teachers offered her a summer job in his bio lab and commuting would be too difficult.

"Look at you, Zach,' Ali said as she hugged me. She stepped back and looked me over. “Man,” she said, “look at all this beautiful hair.”

I hadn’t cut it since my Bar Mitzvah.

She ran her hands through my hair and looked at Jonah.”Shit. Jonah?” Ali hugged him too. “I would have walked right by you guys. Damn, you both grew up fast. And nicely.” She stared at me. “How long has it been? When did I see you last?” Ali was completely wasted. She grabbed my hand and Jonah’s and pulled us along. “Come sit with me and let’s catch up.” She led us to a bench and asked questions about junior high graduation and whether we had girlfriends or not. While we talked, a bunch of Ali’s friends came over. She jumped up excitedly to tell them I was her brother. They looked at me and Jonah without much enthusiasm, but they told Ali to bring us to the party.

“That’s a great idea,” she said. “You must come. It will be cool.” She took each of our hands and pulled us up off the bench. As we caught up with her friends, Ali said, “The party’s in the Village. You’ll come with me and we’ll catch up on the subway, and when we get there I can introduce you to some folks. It’ll be great. It will be magical.”

“I’m not sure,” I said. “We kind of have to get back.”

“For what?”

“Yeah, for what?” Jonah said.

“They’ll be lots of girls,” Ali said.

“We should do what Ali wants,” Jonah said. “I mean it’s been so long since you’ve seen her.”

“Come on Zach. It’s Labor Day and you start high school after this weekend, and I haven’t seen you in so long and here you are showing up at an anti-war gathering. I won’t take no for an answer.”

On the subway, Ali’s friends passed around a sheet of paper that was covered with small pictures of a bearded guy. Each person tore off a picture that they put on their tongues before passing the sheet along. Ali tore off a piece for herself, but not for us. She said we weren’t ready. Another time, she told us.

I must have looked confused.

"It's acid," Ali said. "Blotter. You put it on your tongue and let it melt before swallowing." Ali made us promise to not take any acid if we were offered any at the party.

"Promise me," she said. She looked very serious.

"Are you saying you don't want me to ever do acid?"

"Tonight," she said. "At least for tonight because you're in my care. Okay?"

"Sure."

"You promise."

"We promise," we said, and Ali was all smiles again.

"Pete might be there," Ali said.

"Pete?"

"Seeger. He lives nearby and the guys throwing the party work on festivals and gigs and stuff for him."

"Cool," Jonah said.

Ali locked her arm in mine. She looked at me for a few moments. "I miss Grandpa," she finally said.

"Me too," I exhaled. "Me too. A lot."

"I didn't mean to skip the funeral," Ali said. "It's just that no one told me. I mean it's not their fault. They tried to get a hold of me, but I was no longer crashing at the place they called, and by the time someone reached me it was too late."

"Yeah. We Jews don't waste much time getting rid of the body."

"I used to call Grandpa every week, just to talk. He wanted me to call Mom and Dad, but I told him that I couldn't, and I asked him to keep our calls between us. He said okay. No judgment." Ali rested her head on my shoulder. "Grandpa was special."

"He told me about your calls. He wanted me to know you were okay. He said it was our secret. He was very proud of you. He said you were working to make sure that I didn't have to go to Vietnam."

"You know, Zach, all I care about is pizza and maybe three people. Grandpa was one of them."

I was doing the math and wondering who the others were and if I made the cut. And if I did, well then, who was left out? Our parents?

"It's not three," she said. "It's just a thing I say."

"It's funny," I said.

"You're on the list."

"I'm glad. Not just that I'm on the list, but that it's more than three."

"I borrowed a car one day and went out to see the grave. Kind of felt like I had to say goodbye in person even though I don't actually think he was there – or any part of him. Just his borrowed body left behind. Maybe we let off some tiny bit of energy that rejoins the universe when we die. Maybe we don't. I don't know what I think happens, I just knew I needed to visit the site, to be near his body and say goodbye. Make any sense?"

"Oddly it does," I said.

"He was a good man."

"Mom asked me to be a pallbearer."

"Because Dad couldn't?"

"I guess."

"What was that like?"

"So weird. Possibly the weirdest moment of my life. The whole thing happened in slow motion. I was stoned and sober at the same time. It was the most real and surreal I have ever felt. Then, I literally put Grandpa in the ground and threw dirt on him. How strange is that?"

"Do you remember sitting Shiva for Grandma?" Ali asked. "You had so many questions."

"I was nine."

"So many questions," she added.

"Again," I repeated, "nine."

"He still has a lot of questions," Jonah said as the train made its way past Penn Station.

"I had Grandpa to talk to when Grandma died," I said. "And you."

"I'm sorry," Ali said. "I should have been there for you. I should have been there with you. I should have been there for Grandpa."

• • •

I was in third grade when our Grandma Sara died and Ali and I both missed school for the funeral. We never missed school. When I went to help my father get ready, he asked me if I would go to the cemetery with him. After the service, my mother and her sister went with the casket, and Uncle Herb drove my father with his wheelchair in the trunk and Ali and me in the back seat.

"I wonder what the difference is between a body the moment before and the moment after death," Ali said to me on the ride to the cemetery. "I mean, things stop working, but I wonder if there is anything else that is different."

"What?" I was not following.

"Like where do all those thoughts go? Memories? All that information stored in your brain? Where does that go? There's so much stuff in the brain. Does it just stay there and rot?"

"I don't understand."

"Life and lifeless," Ali pleaded. "Here and gone. Before and after. Living, not living. We are all stardust and we come from the same molecules."

"Now you're just freaking me out," I said.

"Exactly," Ali said.

We laughed.

After the cemetery, we returned to our grandfather's apartment to sit Shiva. The hallway was always dark when you got out of their elevator so when I heard that my grandmother fell, I blamed the darkness, but it turned out she fell in their apartment. That was uncluttered and always well lit. The fall broke her hip, and the hospital broke her spirit. She died there just two days later.

Ali helped our father wash his hands with the pitcher and bowl set in the hallway outside the apartment. I wiped the wheels of his chair. Then we washed our hands.

"We're leaving death outside," our father said.

"Is death here with us now?" I asked.

"What about our shoes or our clothes?" Ali asked.

"Okay," my father smiled. "Yes. it's symbolic. Shiva is about helping us, the living, transition back to life without disrespecting the dead. Symbolism and ritual are useful for that."

Ali held the door and I pushed my father past the threshold.

Inside, a group of women busied themselves arranging everything. They were referred to, unofficially, as the Shiva Sisters. They arrived at the house while the community gathered in the temple. They covered all the mirrors, arranged the food, and made a place for pillows on the floor and against a wall. That was where the mourners, my grandfather and his two daughters, would sit and be able to see everyone coming and going. Sitting lower than their guests, not looking at themselves in mirrors, not changing clothes, they were all part of the process of grieving.

We left our father with his cousin, and Ali and I found our grandfather.

"Grandma wasn't religious," I said.

"Not even a little," he responded.

"So why all this ritual? Did she want it?"

"She liked the traditions, the customs, the community," my grandfather said. "Grandma liked being Jewish even if she had no patience for talk of god. There's comfort in following the same ways as those who came before us," my grandfather added. "This one has merit. You sit for a week. You stop everything. You avoid thinking about yourself and you deal with death head on and then return to life."

"What if it's just a meaningless tradition?" Ali said.

"I have great confidence you will always know the difference."

Ali went off in search of Mrs. Spiegel's chocolate babka, a tradition she found satisfying and meaningful whenever we visited my grandparents' building.

"That's it? You sit Shiva and then you won't miss Grandma?" I asked my grandfather.

"I'll miss her always," he said, pulling on his beard. "Your family on both sides are descendants of Aaron and they started organizing this tradition."

"Moses' brother."

"Yes. Though I think you would have preferred it was Hank Aaron that you descended from."

I laughed because it was true and because I was impressed that my grandfather remembered that I liked Hank Aaron.

"Instead,"he continued, "you are a member of the tribe of Kohanim whose task it was to serve the people as rabbis. To offer the people ideas and explanations and to resolve disputes fairly, consistently, and equitably. You may not become a rabbi, but never stop asking questions. It's the only path to finding answers."

My grandfather was a storyteller and I was his favorite audience. I liked his stories as they were my stories. I was the next chapter he once said to me and then corrected himself and said that I would be starting a new book. He never told me what he meant by that. I loved listening to him talk. The sound of his voice soothed me and wrapped around me like a blanket that made time stop.

Whenever I came over he had a story waiting for me. Or a riddle. There were some stories that my grandfather told me over and over and over when I was young and then later at my request. I could listen to his voice all day. These were his stories, the stories of a life. At first, I did not make the connection between this gray-haired, bearded man who spoke through a thick accent, and the characters of his stories: a child of five, a boy of fourteen, a man at twenty, thirty, forty. I listened and I studied the lines of his forehead, the raising of an eyebrow, the curve of his thick lips, the veins in his hands. He was talking about his life, and these were his stories, his myths, and he was that character working out the plot and clearing roadblocks one scene at a time. It's not easy to grow up, he repeated often. It's even harder to stay young. To not allow age to catch up with us, impossible.

My grandfather took my hand and led me across the room. We stopped next to a woman sitting alone with her back to the room looking out the window.

"Mrs. Bauer, this is my grandson, Zach."

Mrs. Bauer turned around, and I put out my hand as I had been taught. She took my hand and I stared at numbers written on her forearm.

"Be careful," she said to me. "They're back. But this time we won't let them take us. This time we'll be ready."

She turned back to look out the window.

"Auschwitz," my grandfather said when we were out of range. "Seventeen months. Her mother, father shot in front of her in the village square. Her two sisters and brother lost in the gas chambers. You would think that she suffered enough for one lifetime. You might think that, by herself, she has suffered more than all of humanity should ever suffer. And yet she suffers once more. Her mind is crumbling under the weight of its memories, and she sees Nazis everywhere. On the streets, in the supermarket, in the shadows of the noon sun. She lives in constant fear of being taken back to Auschwitz. Is this foolishness? Is she crazy?"

My grandfather paused as Mr. Resnick, who owned the corner deli, brought him a cup of coffee, a prune Danish, and his condolences.

"Is she crazy?" my grandfather repeated after Mr. Resnick left us.

It wasn't a question he wanted me to answer.

"Today we are not openly being hunted down, rounded up, or shipped off. But tomorrow, if she is talking about tomorrow, if she is talking about your lifetime. Your children? Who knows? It's too likely that she's not crazy. Your grandmother and I have always worried about your generation, you and Ali, here in America. Is it prepared to be influenced by Jews? To be infiltrated by Jews? Is America ready and willing to share its power and wealth with its Jews? I hope so, but hope is of little use in such matters. And history has proved otherwise. You must listen to people like Mrs. Bauer. They have paid a high price for what they know. Remember what they have to say and tell it to someone else. And, you must always be ready."

"Ready for what?"

My grandfather looked up at the ceiling and then back at me. He told me about a guard at one of the concentration camps. It may have only been one guard at one camp. It could have been many guards at many camps. The story was always the same – a guard sat in a chair, rifle across his lap, smoking a cigarette, and watched as a handful of Jews, each one a walking skeleton, dug a large hole for a mass grave to bury the gassed. The guard laughed and told the Jews that they would never leave the camp alive. And even if they did, he added, no one would ever believe them when they tried to tell the world what happened.

"Somehow," my grandfather leaned in closer to me, "somehow some of those Jews did make it out. And they did tell their story."

"Like Mrs. Bauer?"

"Yes, like Mrs. Bauer."

I wasn't following everything he said, but I knew he meant every word of it, and I knew it was not the right time for questions. I nodded.

My grandfather leaned in closer to me. "But the SS guard was not completely wrong. There are some who believe none of it happened," he continued. "Do not think, why us? Why Jews? Do not wonder about the killing of your father's parents and all the others. Do not mourn the unborn progeny you never knew. All your missing cousins, aunts, and uncles. Your lost relatives. But, instead, you must never forget them. Always remember that every human on this planet we share has their reason for tears. Here in this country," he continued, "in your country. I don't know if the US will ever really be your country. But here in the US, the stories Native Americans tell are proof of the massacre of their ancestors. Stories passed on by Blacks are proof of slavery, of the willingness of some people to own other people. In much of Europe, Hitler succeeded and there are few Jews left to tell our story, few who have been witness to, who are proof of what happened. Will others tell their stories? Who else will tell our stories? Who will listen to our stories? We need to tell and listen to each other's stories. If we are only interested in our own stories then the holocausts, the genocides, the slaveries, will continue. We must believe that these things happened. Or they will happen again."

"Grandma always said she hated all religion. She said they were the cause of most atrocities."

"She did say all that," my grandfather said. "She hoped for a secular society. I do too. But until then, I am a Jew because the world always reminds me that I am one. These traditions I follow, like Shiva, I follow not because of a god or a holiday or an obligation. Anti-Semitism does not make me feel more Jewish. But I can be against anti-Semitism without becoming religious. Yes, it's not logical. But I am a Jew because I know what happened. And I retell what happened so that it never…that you never, anyone ever has to relive what happened. Telling the story is the only way I know of stopping the story from happening again."

A couple of women brought my grandfather his favorite tea and then left us.

"They know how to throw a good Shiva," he smiled and went to sit on pillows alongside his daughters.

"What are you staring at?" Ali whispered to me. I didn't notice her come up next to me.

"I'm not staring," I said.

"Stop staring," she said. "It's rude."

"I'm not staring at anything."

"You're staring at Mrs. Bauer's numbers. You're starting to freak her out."

"Pretty sure she was already freaked out."

Ali filled a tiny paper cup with some prayer wine and handed it to me. "Drink. It will calm you down."

I told Ali that Grandpa Isaac had to say Kaddish for a month, but our mom had to say it for a year.

"It's longer for kids because while it's possible to replace a husband or wife it's not possible to replace a parent," she told me.

"Do you think that Grandpa will get remarried?" I asked Ali.

"Why not?" she said. "But isn't this a little early to be thinking about that?"

He never did remarry, but he did seem to visit Mrs. Spiegel and her chocolate babka in apartment 4B an awful lot. He called her his special friend.

• • •

"You know how Grandma and Grandpa always kept their passports handy?" I said to Ali as the train came to a stop on 14th Street.

"Sure," she said. "Right near the door where they kept their keys. It was like they always wanted to be ready to leave."

"Well, I took them when I went with Mom to help her clear things out of his apartment. I took his and Grandma's."

"Okay," Ali said as we followed her up the stairs onto 6th Avenue. "Mom didn't care?"

"Mom didn't know."

"Do you know why you took them?"

"I do not," I said. "I just felt like I needed to."

"I'm glad you did," Ali said.

I was thinking about the passports as we emerged on the street. Would I be ready to leave the US at a moment's notice? Maybe being ready was my part. Maybe that was what my grandfather had been trying to get me to understand without telling me. Sure, Israel was around now, but if the Holocaust was any lesson it was that the Jew haters didn't just want us to leave. They wanted us dead. So finding a way to escape, finding a way out, being ready to leave was a necessity. Maybe that was my job. Even though my parents knew all about fleeing. Still, I had to do my part if it came to that. Or maybe it was better to be thinking WHEN it came to that.

Ali and I made a deal that I would call her every other Wednesday from Jonah's house. I liked knowing she was safe. She was walking between Jonah and me, took our hands in hers, and started skipping. She pulled us along as we turned west on 12th Street.

"Wait." I stopped. "You live near that house that blew up?"

"Yeah. It's around the corner," she said.

"Did you know them?"

"No, Zach, I didn't know them. I don't get involved with that kind of crap."

"That shit sucks," I said. "Your friends don't do that, do they?"

"They were making pipe bombs in the basement. They were going to set off those bombs in random public places and kill innocent people." Suddenly she didn't sound high at all. More pissed. "Why would you think I would be any part of that?"

"I was just worried."

"That would make me a thug like the people we're trying to stop."

"He gets like this," Jonah said. "It's annoying."

"Yeah," Ali said. Then she turned to me. "Listen, little brother, it's cool you're serious. Just not all the time. Not tonight. Tonight is a fun night. Who says the revolution can't be a party."

"Not me," Jonah said.

"Fuck yeah," I said, marshalling enthusiasm.

Ali herded us up the steps to the apartment. "Zach, Jonah. Your job is to have fun. Also, tell the girls you're in college," she said. And with that, she led us inside.

Jonah and I made our way into the kitchen and found some beer and a telephone. We found a number for Tony's grandmother and told him where we were. He said he and Mel would walk over after they finished dinner.

I was surprised to see these two guys in army jackets. They were standing on either side of a girl with long brown hair. She was wearing a cool jean jacket. One of the army coats was wearing aviator glasses even though it was dark inside. The other guy had a piercing stare that was fixed on me. All three of them were headed our way. I guess I had been staring. I couldn't stop, even as they got closer.

"Is your friend okay?" the girl asked.

"He's not," Jonah said.

"Marine?" I asked the guy with the aviator glasses. He had two tags, a rectangular silver one and a round bronze one and I was trying to read them. I'd seen pictures.

"Zach is a bit obsessed," Jonah said. Then he elbowed me.

"Was," he said. "Staff Sergeant Frank Tinelli, United States Marine Corps. You can call me Frankie."

"How did you know he was a Marine?" the girl asked.

"His tags have his gas mask size and blood type. Only Marines list their gas mask size," I said.

"Damn straight," Frankie said. "What about my buddy Sal?"

Sal dug dog tags out from under his shirt and showed them to me.

"Also Marine," I said.

"Corporal Sal Marino. Proud to have served alongside my brother, Staff Sergeant Tinelli," he said, saluting me. Then he yelled out, "Semper Fi," to no one in particular.

The kitchen went silent for a moment.

"He's cute," the girl said to Frankie.

"And this lovely lady is Sunny," Frankie said.

"I'm Jonah, and he's Zach."

"Served?" I asked. "Where?

"We're going out back to smoke a joint," Sal said. "You're welcome to join us."

"That's cool," Jonah said, as we followed them down the hallway. He was staring at me like he did when he wanted me to stop asking questions.

Once outside, Frankie lit a joint and offered it to me. "Have a hit off this."

"Thanks, man," I said as I held it between my thumb and index finger.

"It's really strong," Sunny warned.

"A special stash," Sal said.

I held the joint to my lips and sucked. The tip lit up brightly and created a cloud of smoke that caused my nose to lift up like an infield fly. Their pot didn't just smell, it stunk. It literally smelled like crap. But it was smooth and warm and didn't taste anything like it smelled.

"What kind of grass is this?" Jonah asked.

"That there," Frankie said, "is pure Hanoi gold."

"Outstanding," I said through exhaled smoke and passed the joint to Jonah.

"Straight from the jungles of Vietnam," Sal added.

"This pot was in Vietnam?" I asked. "Were you in Vietnam? That's where you served?"

"Boots on the ground to wheels up, thirteen months," Frankie said. "Three hundred and ninety-six days. Me and Sal together."

Sal lit a cigarette and inhaled like he was trying to suck it all the way down in one breath. He exhaled and threw it down, stepping on it as he started pacing. Sunny jumped off the bench and put her arms around him and whispered something. I wasn't sure what was happening, but he stopped pacing. Then she kissed him on the cheek. Frankie threw his arm around Sal's neck and handed him the joint.

"I never met anyone who's been in Vietnam," I said. "I don't even know anyone who knows someone who's been in Vietnam. The guys in our neighborhood, they all get college deferments."

"That's coming to an end," Frankie said.

"Yeah," I said. I kind of felt like I should stop asking questions. But I didn't. "What was it like?"

Jonah gave me that look again.

"Are you thinking of becoming a Marine?" Frankie asked.

"Oh no," I responded, a little too fast and a little too loud. Everyone laughed, and then I did too. "No disrespect to the Marines. I'm in favor of Marines. It's the war I'm not in favor of."

"No offense taken," Frankie said. "We shouldn't be there."

"Nobody wants us to be, " Sal said.

"Not even the South Vietnamese?" Jonah asked.

"Not the people, no. Unless they're making money off the war," Frankie said. "The hawks are all about the scratch."

"We're never going to win." Sal lit another cigarette and paced around in circles.

"Light us up another," Frankie handed Jonah a joint.

"You sure?" I asked.

"We're just getting started," Frankie said.

"I meant, are you sure we can't win," I said.

"Yes. I'm sure," Sal said. "I'm fucking sure." He began pacing again. "You want to know how I know?"

"Sure," I said. Then I saw the way Sunny looked at me. Like I shouldn't have asked.

Sal inhaled his cigarette slow and deep. Then he exhaled quickly, like a runner trying to work out a side sticker. A cloud rose around him. He sucked on his cigarette again, sat down on the steps and started talking about how they were sent in to sweep a village during Tet.

"You were in country during Tet?" I asked.

Frankie quickly put his hand on my shoulder and shook his head. "No questions. Just listen."

"Not so much a village as a few thatch-roofed huts," Sal went on. "We'd been in and out of choppers all week chasing VC, but they always knew we were coming and hid in their tunnels. They had fucking tunnels everywhere. We finished up, and the choppers had come to get us. We're climbing into the Cobras to get airlifted back to base. We had R and R coming. As we're taking off, this guy, more like some kid. He's in black PJs. Anyway, this kid, he appears out of the bush and starts shooting arrows at us. From a crossbow. Fucking arrows. Who the hell shoots arrows at Cobras?"

"No one," Frankie said.

"That's right," Sal said. "No. Fucking. One." Sal took a few drags off his cigarette. "You'd have to be crazy."

"Completely. Totally. Certifiable," Frankie echoed.

"Did you shoot him? The guy with the arrows?" I asked.

Sunny looked at me and shook her head. I had gone too far. Sal started pacing again. Frankie jumped up and stood next to Sal who stopped moving.

"Fucking arrows," I said.

Sal laughed. "Fucking arrows. Far fucking out." He turned and looked directly at me. I froze. "So now you tell me. How are you going to defeat a people who are willing to face down that kind of firepower with crossbows and arrows."

I wasn't sure if he wanted me to answer, but he kept staring at me, and he had a crazed look in his eyes. I whispered, "You're not."

"Damn straight," he said, smiling and slapping my shoulder.

"I like this kid," Sal said.

I exhaled. Frankie hopped back onto the steps and sat below Sunny who threw her arms around his neck and kissed the top of his head. He kept his gaze on Sal.

"We should drop this pot all over Vietnam," Jonah said. "That would start a cease-fire."

"I like your thinking," Sal said, coming back to the stoop. "I can dig that," he said to Jonah.

"How old are you?"

"Thirteen," I said. "Jonah is fourteen."

"But we're starting high school. Sophomores."

"You're too young to worry about this stuff," Sunny said.

"You have plenty of time," Frankie said.

I wanted to ask, time for what? But Sal started talking.

"You guys live around here?" Sal asked.

"Queens," I said.

"Cool," he said. "We grew up near here. East Village. Alphabet city."

"The day we graduated, we enlisted," Sal said. "Together."

"Bronx Science," Frankie said.

"You could have gone to college, but you enlisted?" I asked.

"Pretty dumb," Sal said.

"Listen," Frankie said. "If this crap is still happening when you get drafted, don't go."

I looked at him. "I don't understand."

"If we're dumb enough to still be in Vietnam," Sal said, putting his hands on my shoulders and staring at me. "Look, maybe there was a time, maybe. But I doubt it. But maybe there was a time long ago when it was cool, even noble, to die for one's country. But if there was a time, it's gone. All there is now is dying. That's it. Dying like a dog and for no reason at all. Just dying. So you must not go. You must not get on that conveyor belt that's feeding the war machine with bodies of America's best men."

"We enlisted and we were wrong," Frankie said. His eyes were locked in on Jonah and me. He was making me nervous. "We could have had fucking deferments, and we enlisted." Frankie pulled out a bandana and wiped his forehead. "That decision was like throwing a fucking pebble in a lake. It's easy to make the water ripple. But you can't make it stop." He looked back at Sal's before reaching into his pocket for another cigarette. "It's impossible to make it stop."

"Like you might just need to answer nature's call so you break bush, and just like that a punji stake rips your thigh," Sal said. He was speaking to himself mostly at this point.

"A what?"

"A booby trap with a bamboo stick that has shit, real shit all over it. Leaves an awful infection."

"Fucking Paulie," Frankie said, looking at Sal. I think he wanted, needed, Sal's approval or confirmation. "At least he got to go home early."

"With one less testicle."

"Sal, honey," Sunny said."They're just kids."

"Madness and sadness, man," Frankie said to no one. He hopped off the steps. "Madness and sadness." Seemed like his mind was somewhere else.

"No more sadness, honey. You're home now." Sunny rose after Frankie and wrapped her arms around him in a bear hug. She stroked his hair.

"Isn't it wrong to let others go in my place?" I asked.

Frankie turned and stared at me.

"Stop talking about the war," Jonah whispered to me.

Frankie's stare turned into a huge grin. "I knew this kid was okay."

Sunny smiled at me, but I wasn't following. But I didn't care because hanging with them was cool.

"You guys play baseball?" Frankie asked.

"Yeah," we both said.

"Jonah's really good," I said.

"It's a great game because everyone gets the same twenty-seven outs," Frankie said.

"And there's no clock," I added.

"And the object of the game is to get home," Frankie said. "That's all anyone is fighting for over there. Just trying to get back home. In one piece."

"But life isn't fair like baseball," Sal added. "The clock starts as soon as you're born and not everyone gets to play all nine innings."

Frankie reached into his jacket and pulled out a cigarette. "Sunny's right," he said.

"About what?" Sunny asked.

"Sunny is always right," Sal said.

"Don't worry about any of this now," Frankie said. "Go to high school and get high, meet girls. And study. Study hard and get fucking smart so you can figure out how to stop wars from happening. We're not smart enough for that."

"Definitely find a girl," Sal chimed in.

"You guys are cute," Sunny said. "Girls will go crazy for you."

"Listen, our families are throwing a party in honor of us being discharged," Frankie said. "So we should be heading back."

"They must be glad you're home," I said.

"They are. As long as we don't talk about Vietnam," Frankie said.

"They don't want to know anything that happened."

"The thing is," Sal said, "you come home and the only people who have any idea what you went through are your brothers, and for everyone else, there's no way to describe it. Yeah, I could tell you funny stories. I could tell you horror tales. I could tell you tales of heroism. I could tell you stories that would make you piss yourself. Or I could try to tell you how the men we served with are the best, the very best people we will ever know. But none of that would be even close to describing what it was like in country."

Sal looked at Frankie.

"Too many of our brothers have come back without all of their faculties intact," Frankie said. "Too many have not come back at all. So we get that we're the lucky ones. But nothing we could tell our parents would help them understand what we went through. Nothing we could tell anyone begins to explain what we did. What we had to do. How we lived. Just can't be told. That's why we brought Sunny," Frankie said. "To distract our parents."

"To distract us," Sal said.

"Your parents mean well," Sunny said. "They just can't bear to hear what their babies endured."

"Frankie's mom, she made me her sausage lasagna," Sal said. "The one with five different flavored sausages. I am going to go to town on that."

"It's a mystery why my mom loves you," Frankie said, putting his arm around Sal.

"No mystery," Sal said. "I'm me."

Frankie gave Jonah two joints and told him to save them for another day.

Sunny hugged me. I was not expecting that. Her breasts felt so good against my chest and her hair smelled amazing.

"Remember what they told you," Sunny whispered in my ear. "They know." She kissed my cheek. "Listen and remember."

I felt completely distracted.

Then she hugged Jonah.

"How cool was that hug?" I said to Jonah after they left.

"Don't talk."

"She felt so good," I said.

"You felt her?" Jonah laughed.

"I mean it felt great."

"We need girlfriends," Jonah said.

"Yes, please," I said. "At least you had Steph."

"Had is the key word."

We headed back inside to the party and listened to music while the pot did its thing. After a few songs, I said I wanted to look for Ali.

"I liked Steph, but she's no Ali," Jonah said. "Ali is so cool. I should ask her out."

"Why would you bring up my sister and ruin this moment for me?"

"She danced with me at your Bar Mitzvah," Jonah said.

"That was a year ago, and you wouldn't stop asking her," I said. "You're killing my high."

"Would it be weird to have me for a brother-in-law? Considering I'm already your brother."

"You mean like incest?" I said.

"If Ali and I had a kid would he be your nephew or your brother?

"Nobody's having any babies. Especially not you and Ali," I said.

"Speaking of having sex, you need to hurry up and get laid," Jonah said.

"I'm working on it."

"Work harder. We've always done new shit together," he lamented.

"At the same time," I said.

"What did I say?"

"You said together. This is something we want to do at the same time, not together."

Jonah said he was going to look for food. I said I wasn't hungry and instead I followed the music into a crowded room. There was space against the wall and I leaned back and listened. First, there was a guy who played an acoustic guitar and sang some Sam Cooke songs. Another guy accompanied him on harmonica.

They did a few songs together and then this girl took over. She played guitar and sang. She told a story about each song she wrote before she played it.

I had been standing there for some time and my mouth was feeling very dry. I thought I would look for something to drink and at that moment Tony and Mel walked in. I told them that we got high with some Vietnam Veterans.

"It's hard to tell if you're more excited about how good the pot was or that you got high with some vets," Tony said.

"They gave Jonah some of their Vietnam stash," I said.

"We should find Jonah then," Mel said.

We found Jonah sitting at the kitchen table eating spaghetti. When he saw us he smiled.

"This is the best spaghetti I ever tasted," Jonah said. "Topanga here, she made it for me. How cool is that?"

"Very," I said.

"You must have some," Topanga said. "You must all have some."

"That's all right," I said. "I'm not hungry. Just thirsty."

"We just had dinner," Tony said.

I drank some orange juice while Topanga told us about being a student at Cooper Union and about how she grew up in Chicago. And how she lived in the house so it was kind of her party.

"We should let you two eat," Mel said.

That was my cue to get a joint from Jonah. I told Mel and Tony to follow me out back. But I needed to pee so I gave them the joint and told them I'd meet them. As I stood over the bowl, I thought about how much we relied on indoor plumbing. New York City would become uninhabitable if the system shut down. It's like the more civilization advanced, the more vulnerable it became.

I left the bathroom and was immediately tackled in the narrow hallway.

"Stay down," the guy on top of me yelled as he pressed me into the floor.

I had no problem staying down. I had a problem moving any part of me, so I just lay there with my nose pressed against the floor. That's when I heard a girl talking to the guy on top of me.

"Look at me David," she repeated. "Look at me. It's Samm." She touched my shoulder. "Are you okay?"

"Great," I said.

"Just stay still for a second and we'll get him off of you."

"No problem. Not like I can move." I heard her laugh.

"What's your name?"

"Zach."

"He thinks you're in his unit, Zach," Samm told me.

"Unit?"

"Vietnam," she said. "He's trying to protect you."

"From who?" I asked.

"The Viet Cong."

"Right," I said. "That's a good thing?"

Samm was able to coax David off me and I sat up, leaning against the hallway wall. Someone handed me a soda, and Samm told me that David was having a bad flashback.

"Are there good flashbacks?" I asked. The wall seemed very safe.

"Probably not," Samm said.

"We need to find cover," David said to me. "It's not safe here."

"You're safe here. We're safe, David," Samm told him.

A couple of guys came over and sat on the floor with David. They were telling him that he was in Manhattan. He was no longer in country. They kept repeating that he was back in *The World* and that he was safe.

"We were never safe," David said. His head was turning back and forth like he was keeping watch, as if monitoring everyone coming and going through the hallway.

The guys told David that they were going to help him up and wanted to take him outside to get some air. One of them turned to me and told me that I had to go first.

"Me?" I wasn't sure why I had to go first or go at all.

"David needs to see that you are safe," Samm told me. She offered me her hand and I took it. We walked slowly, avoiding sudden movements that might get me tackled again. I slipped ahead and opened the back door which led to a small patio that led to a smaller yard. David and those two guys followed with Samm walking backward, facing David and speaking softly to him, trying to calm him. They helped David settle down onto the cement stoop where they kept trying to convince him that the war, at least for him, was over.

Seemed to me that the war was far from over for David. Seemed to me that it might never be over for him.

"Jerome is gone," David said.

"You're not in the jungle anymore, David," Samm said.

"We'd been in and out of the jungle for months, so it was no big deal," David said. "It wasn't the first time I drew the short straw and walked point."

"You don't have to remember all this David," Samm said.

"I do have to. Someone has to, or we'll all forget and no one will believe it happened."

"I'll believe you David," Samm said. "I will always believe you."

"Jerome was only nineteen. It was a long patrol, and I thought it would never end. The kind of patrol that had a strange mix of mind-numbing boredom and mind-blowing anxiety knowing that every step could be your last. All I could do was try to focus on something else, on anything else. We were all itching to break the tedium. That's when we came under fire. Jerome was behind me. He yelled for us to get down and then he was gone. He was only nineteen. I'm looking at him now. And then Daniel, he kicked a land mine and it took his leg off and he's lying there screaming, 'god help us all' until the medics shoot him up with morphine to ease the pain and because every VC within a mile can hear him and are shooting in his direction. Which is our direction. It took four days for the choppers to land and get us out. By then there were only seven of us left. Daniel didn't make it. We hadn't slept, and were out of food and water and down to a few hundred rounds of ammo that we'd been taking from our dead brothers. Daniel, he was short by a couple of weeks. Supposed to go back to Brooklyn at the end of August. They sent him home early. In a bag. I went to see his mom. She told me it was the same day Armstrong stepped on the moon."

"The war is over for Jerome and Daniel," Samm said. "But it's not your fault."

"But I see them. I always see them. And Daniel, he won't stop screaming. It's not safe to scream in the jungle."

Samm sat next to David and put her arm around his shoulder and rocked him from side to side.

"I can't unsee what I've seen, Samm," David said. "I can't unknow what I know. And I can't undo what I did."

Samm started crying. "It's not your fault," David.

"What does it all mean, man?"

"I don't know," Samm said. "I don't know. I wish I did, but I don't."

"No one does," one of the guys said.

"But we love you," Samm said. "You have to know that we do." She kissed his cheek.

"Why can't I sleep? How come the doctors can't tell me why this rash won't go away?"

"I don't know," Samm said

The two guys told Samm that they were going to take David with them and wait out the acid trip. Samm made David promise to visit.

"Tell mom and dad I'm sorry," David said.

"Sorry for what?"

"For coming home a mess."

"They're just glad you're home, David."

"I need to get back to camp," he said standing up. "That's where I'm safe. With the others."

"Okay, David," Samm said as everyone stood up. "No more needles. And you have to promise to call me."

Samm slumped down on the ground after they left. "Are you okay?" Samm asked me. "He hit you pretty hard."

"How long was he in Nam?"

"Two tours. He was discharged, but he's thinking about re-upping."

"Why?" I said too quickly, but she didn't notice.

"He says his life makes sense there. That he doesn't know how to live here anymore. He doesn't know what to do, how to act."

"What's the camp? What did he mean by that?"

"He's probably thinking about Vietnam."

"I thought one of the guys said they were going to a place called Vung Tau Base?"

"That's in Vietnam," Samm said. "It's where David went for R and R. There's a beach there," Samm said. "Can we not talk for a moment?"

"Okay," I said. "Should I leave?"

"Can you sit next to me? Can we just sit here and not talk?"

"Sure," I said as I sat.

"Can you hold me?"

I put my arm around her, and we sat in silence for several minutes. I wasn't sure if she was crying, but I didn't ask, and I didn't move my arm.

"I'm fifteen," Samm said, breaking the silence, but not moving.

"That's a bit random"

"I got involved with these guys around anti-war stuff. I make sure they know that I'm under eighteen."

"Why?" I asked. "Wait. Never mind."

Samm laughed. I liked hearing her laugh.

"You're in college," I asked, "and you're only fifteen? How smart are you?"

"Who said I was in college?"

"Ali said everyone was in college."

"How do you know Ali?"

"She's my sister."

"Really?" Samm said, processing that new information. She freed herself from my arm and looked at me. "Interesting."

"Why?"

"Ali's like the smartest chick I ever met. Are you in college?"

"No," I said without thinking. So much for Ali's plan.

"So, not everyone."

"I guess not," I laughed.

"What grade are you in?"

"I'm going to be a sophomore."

"Me too," Samm said. "How old are you?"

"I'm fifteen like you."

"I'm fourteen," Samm said.

"Me too."

"Cool."

"And I'll be fourteen in a month," I said and instantly regretted it. I'm not sure why I thought I should tell her. We had already settled on fourteen.

"Okay." Samm stood.

"Okay, what?" I said nervously.

"Okay, thanks for being honest with me even though I know you want to sleep with me," she said.

"I don't. I mean, of course, yeah, but, I didn't. I mean, it's not what I was thinking right now." I stopped talking. Samm just sat there smiling at me. "I'm going to just go with, you're welcome."

"I think you better." Samm kissed my cheek. "Thank you, Zach.

"For what?"

"For helping out with David."

"You're welcome."

"But now I need to go."

"Go?"

"Leave."

"Because of how old I am?"

"Because I need to get home."

"I'll go with you," I offered.

"That's sweet, but no."

"What if I want to anyway?"

"It's not up to you," she laughed.

"I like you," I said. "I want to see you again."

"You should."

"I should like you, or I should want to see you again?"

"Both," Samm said.

"Where do you live? What's your phone number."

"You'll have to find me."

"I thought I just did."

"Then do it again. Meet me under the clock in the Biltmore next Saturday. Five o'clock." And then Samm kissed me on my cheek again. "Find me," she said as she turned and disappeared into the house.

On the ride home, I told everyone about what happened but mostly about Samm and how I couldn't wait to see her again. They were all very high. Queens was quiet by the time the four of us emerged from the subway. Tony and Mel crossed Queens Boulevard toward Mel's apartment and Jonah and I made our way up 63rd Drive. By the time we turned on to Alderton we were the only ones out. I was telling Jonah how cool Samm was when suddenly a car came out of nowhere and pulled up next to us, slowing down and driving alongside us as we walked. There were four guys in the car and the ones on our side rolled down their windows and started shouting and swearing at us.

I recognized two of them. The G brothers. George and Griff. Well known neighborhood bullies. It was like their job and they seemed to take it seriously. I guess every neighborhood had its bullies and these assholes were ours. The guy riding shotgun threw a bottle at us and we took off running.

Suddenly Jonah started singing, "We're not going to make it," like that Who song from Tommy and I started singing too except that's not the words, and we're just repeating that one line cause it's hard to think when you're laughing and scared and running all at the same time. Then the car stopped. And we stopped singing. And they opened their car doors and we started running faster.

"Come on," Jonah said. "Follow me." He turned and ran up the steps of the random house we were in front of. I followed. Jonah pulled out his keys and opened the screen door like it was our house and we both stood there looking at the bully brothers who were drunk. Maybe it was the number of steps between us, or maybe the threat of us going inside and calling the cops, but they lost interest and got back in their car and peeled off after new prey. We sat at the bottom of the steps and caught our breath before heading home.

"How did you come up with that line while we were running?" I said, standing in the middle of the street between our houses.

"I think someone was playing that song at the party and it just popped into my head. We're not going to make it seem obvious."

"Outstanding," I said, hugging Jonah.

"This was a good night," Jonah said.

"The best."

And with that, we each turned toward our houses and our bedrooms and our beds.

But I wasn't tired. I had just met a girl.

SOMETHING IN THE AIR

My new math teacher, Mr. Steel, had long pony-tailed hair that stood out among the other teachers at the incoming sophomore orientation assembly. Word quickly spread through the auditorium that he drove the VW van in the teacher's parking lot and that he was working on a math Ph.D. at CCNY. A rumor was going around that he had a deferment. Something about 4E or F.

Ever since I could solve quadratic equations in sixth grade, teachers started assigning me extra math work – even before I knew they were doing it. So, that was how my schedule had me in AP Calculus. Unlike other subjects, they allowed multiple grades in the same math class which put me with two juniors and nine seniors. Ten guys and two girls.

I had always thought math was limited to answers, to solutions. Mr. Steel said we would be spending the year considering how much more it could be. He wanted us to retroactively think of algebra as the math of operations, and geometry as the math of shapes. Calculus, he said, our subject, was the math of change. Mathematics, he proclaimed, could explain everything. Everything, he repeated.

Everything? I'd been looking for answers to everything. I hadn't found answers to anything.

Turned out that Mr. Steel was also a lifelong suffering Mets fan. He showed us the small transistor radio and earpiece he kept inside his desk to listen to Mets games during school. He promised that if they did manage to get into the playoffs for the first time in their history then we would listen to any games that were played during class time.

High school had brought a lot of changes for me and Jonah, but the biggest change, the most surprising, was happening a few miles away in Shea Stadium where the Mets were still playing games that mattered so late in the season. Well, that's not entirely true. The fact that I had a date with Samm, that I had a date with anyone, was just astonishing. It's just that Jonah and I had been waiting for the Mets to make the playoffs longer than we knew we wanted girlfriends.

As he talked, Mr. Steel walked around collecting the index cards we had written our names on. He shuffled them before randomly dealing two cards to a desk. The location of our cards would indicate our assigned seat. The two students whose cards paired them to the same desk would be study partners for the year. I tried to play it cool as I had won the lottery being paired with Lisa, a senior and one half of the female population of the class. Was it possible that Mr. Steel was that adult who was worth listening to? After all, calculus was all about sines and cosines so maybe that too was a sign.

"You think they'll actually make the playoffs?" Lisa said as she picked up my hat.

"Ever been to Shea?" I asked. I wanted to know what she knew.

"Sure. We used to come down a few times a year."

"Come down?"

"I'm new here," Lisa said.

"New from?"

"Nyack." Lisa tried on my hat. It looked great on her. She pulled the brim down, blocking her eyes like pitchers do.

"You're a Mets fan?" I asked.

"Mostly because of my dad."

"How did you get into baseball?"

"You mean because I'm a girl?"

"I didn't notice," I said.

"That's funny," Lisa laughed.

"And because you're not from Queens."

"Nice recovery," she said. "When I was little, my dad and I would listen to games on the radio. One day he took out this beautiful book and taught me to keep score. If he had to work late he'd get me to listen to the game and keep the scorebook. I'd go over the play by play with him in the morning."

"You do know that they put box scores in the papers?" I said, thinking how cool it was that she could share baseball with her dad.

"I do now, but that's still not play-by-play," she laughed. "I was six."

"So you are a Mets fan."

"I want them to win for him," she said. "It would make him happy. He deserves some of that."

Your dad and every other Mets fan, I thought. "What about your mom?"

"She was also a Mets fan."

"Was? Don't tell me she became a Yankee fan."

"No. Not a Yankee fan," Lisa stopped talking and looked away and didn't say anything.

My mind raced with all the other reasons Lisa might have used past tense. None of them had to do with baseball and none of them seemed like a good thing.

When she turned back toward me, Lisa quietly said, "She died last year."

"That sucks," I said before I could think.

Lisa tilted her head back so I could see her whole face. She stared at me like that for a few very long moments. I was too scared to look away. Too scared to say anything.

"No one ever says that," she said.

"I'm sorry." It only took me like five minutes to insult her. I was so screwed.

"It does suck," she said. "It sucks a whole lot." She smiled and her whole face changed.

I started breathing again.

• • •

The following Saturday I packed for a sleepover and headed to Jonah's where his dad let me in, but as usual, he didn't say anything to me. I went upstairs to Jonah's room and tossed my bag on the guest bed, which had been basically my second bed since forever. I liked that his mom made my bed with Jonah's old sheets from when we were kids. It was cowboy sheets that day. My favorite.

I put The Doors on Jonah's record player and dropped the needle onto "People Are Strange." I sat on the floor and listened.

Jonah's sister came into the room. "Where's Jonah?" Wendy asked while Jim Morrison began singing about the different ways people are strange.

"Showering."

Wendy opened Jonah's desk drawer and moved things around until she found his wallet. She removed a ten dollar bill which she pushed into her jean shorts. Then she removed a condom from Jonah's wallet and looked at it. "I heard he was screwing some ninth-grader," she said and slipped it back in and replaced the wallet in the drawer. "How about you? You still a virgin?" Wendy picked up my Jimi Hendrix t-shirt from my bed. I was glad it distracted her. "It'll happen," she said. And just like that she turned her back to me and pulled off her shirt. She wasn't wearing anything under it and she didn't seem to care what I saw. She slipped on my Hendrix shirt and stood in front of Jonah's mirror. "That's what high school is for," she said turning to me. "Is this yours?"

"Yeah." I had planned to wear it that night.

"Let me borrow it, okay?" she said.

"Sure." I'm pretty sure it didn't matter what I said. It looked good on her. Better than on me.

"Tell Jonah I took ten dollars," she said on her way out.

Wendy was two years older than Jonah and me, but with SP we were catching up to her in school and we were now sophomores during her junior year. She and Jonah were never that close, but she was never mean to us. She scared me a little, which Jonah thought was funny. She always paid back the money she took, even when she didn't tell him.

"Where do you think you're going?" I heard Jonah's dad yelling at Wendy. "You still live in my house, young lady." He went on to tell her how he didn't like her boyfriend. This was a new boyfriend, but not a new argument. I'd heard him say it about every one of her boyfriends. Wendy went out with older guys. Had since junior high. As Wendy made it clear to her father that he would not have to put up with her much longer, I turned up the volume and let The Doors loose.

• • •

Jonah and I slipped out of the house without seeing his father. When we reached Queens Boulevard, we turned left at Danny's Deli where they had those amazing sour pickles that came from that guy on Delancey. We walked past the shoe store, the old bakery, and the new liquor store. We picked up some rolling papers from Further Records and headed to the schoolyard.

The plan was for me to meet up with Jonah at the schoolyard later in the evening after my date with Samm and then go back to his house. On 67th, I kept going to the subway while Jonah turned toward the schoolyard.

I transferred to the F Train and took it to 42nd Street. I made my way up to 6th Avenue and entered Bryant Park. Whenever I was anywhere close, I liked to walk through the big library. Bryant Park, which was in the back of the massive library, was home to a seedy side of New York. As I strolled through it toward the building's rear entrance, hookers and dealers and scammers made their pitches.

"Hey, baby, you got a girlfriend?"

"Loose joints?" Coke?"

"You looking for some fun, white boy?"

I kept a straight face and didn't make eye contact. After all, they were working, and I wouldn't want to waste their time or interfere with the way they did their jobs.

I entered the library and made my way to the lobby. I liked the main branch because of all of its special rooms and special books, and those long wooden tables and lamps. But also because it was truly a public place – the town square – a place where everyone had equal access to all of the city's documents and information.

I loved the main room with its ritual of filling out a request form that I personally handed to a librarian behind the long counter. I liked following its path as the note was placed in a cylinder that was sucked into a tube which I imagined winding its way through a labyrinth of floors and hallways and corridors toward the correct location. At journey's end, the note was retrieved by a hidden librarian who used the scribbled call numbers to locate the precise row and stack and shelf that held my book or magazine. If it was found shelved, my item was then placed into a larger tube that sent the item back to the main desk where my name was called, and I would be granted temporary use. Just like that. Well, not just like that. It wasn't the fastest process. But I didn't care. The librarians were like guides and the big room was where I went to find out about stuff. Like whether men with polio were able to make babies.

Taxes paid for my entrance and use of this building. And taxes also paid for parks and roads and bridges and tunnels. They paid for my school, too. And they paid for the war. I guess the issue wasn't taxes, but choices. How do we make the right choices? And who do we allow to make those choices for us?

I pushed on the doors in the rotunda and stepped out onto the library's landing high above 5th Avenue. I skipped down the steps between the two stone lions, Patience and Fortitude. After crossing the busy street, I made my way into Grand Central Station where I followed the tiled tunnel to the Biltmore Hotel. As it gave lovers a direct link to the hotel, it was called the Tryst Tunnel.

I arrived early to avoid being late. Samm was not in the crowd gathered in the lobby under the clock. I stayed inside because outside were protesters who wanted the hotel's male-only bar to allow women, and I didn't want to be that male they got mad at.

I took one of the cushy chairs in the lobby and acted as if I belonged. I watched as men and women nervously, impatiently, eagerly, nonchalantly waited under the clock for their rendezvous to show up. I started trying to guess who they were, what their jobs were, who was married, who was having an affair, who was on a first date, and who was about to have sex. I realized it was possible to be all of those at once. Which led me to wonder how much a room cost for one night. Could that be why Samm wanted to meet me in the lobby? Then I wondered how dumb I could be. That answer was easy. Very.

Samm pushed through the heavy glass doors and I stood up and walked toward her. "You made it," I said.

"You sound surprised,"

I hugged Samm. "I might be." I really might have been.

"You didn't think I would show?"

"Let's just say I'm happy to see you."

We left the hotel and turned north toward Radio City. Suddenly Samm stopped. She bent to pick up a penny. Only she didn't pick it up. She flipped it over and left it on the sidewalk where she found it.

"What's that about?" I asked as she stood.

"It's this thing my friend Elbee started. Whenever we see a penny that's face-up, we pick it up for good luck. But if the penny is face down," she continued, "we flip it over and leave it for the next person to find it, so they can have good luck."

"What if someone sees a face down penny and picks it up?"

"Not our problem," Samm said. "According to Elbee, we are only responsible for the pennies we see. If we flip those, then we did our part."

"Elbee?"

"Last name."

"What does Elbee do with a quarter or a dollar?"

"She keeps those. It's only for pennies," Samm said.

"Why?"

"Because Elbee said only pennies are lucky and it's her game, so it's her rules."

"Cool. But the game is totally weird. Does Elbee actually believe in the luck granting power of her pennies?"

A wedding was spilling out on Fifth Avenue, up ahead at Saint Peter's Cathedral.

"She says she has proof."

"Proof?" We stopped across the street from St. Peter's and watched as the wedding party threw rice on the bride and groom. Most were missing their target.

"Not so much proof as she believes in things not seen."

"So she hopes it's true?"

"Nothing wrong with hope. It just may be our best thing," Samm said.

"I hope not."

Samm laughed.

I was about to say that all hope is false. Instead, I stopped myself.

"Elbee's game is cool," I said.

"I'll be *sure* to tell her."

"I deserve that." I said, wondering if I'd blown it with Samm.

The bride and groom got into a limo decorated with the usual streamers and "4 EVER" written in soap on the back windshield.

"Is forever only for when you're on earth?" I said.

"What?"

I pointed at the limo.

"Explain," Samm said.

"It's till death do us part, right?"

"Right."

"So after death parts them, are all bets off? What if you have a second wife because your first one died. And the second wife has a dead husband. Who gets to be with who in heaven? Death parted all of them but not in any particular order."

"I guess you get to have an orgy?"

"See, Jews don't believe in an afterlife. But if we were sure about the orgy thing, you might see more converts."

A few blocks later we entered Central Park where Samm took me to see the ducks. We sat on the rocks and were silent for a while. She seemed sad.

"David used to take me here," she said. "My mom always saved old bread for us." Samm stood and I jumped up and followed her. "I haven't heard from him since he left the party. I'm not sure where he is, but he said he wanted to go back to Vietnam. He doesn't have to go. He wants to. I'm worried about him. He's not okay. He says he's better over there, but how could Vietnam be a better place for him. You saw him, I hope he'll come home before he reenlists."

"Do you want to try to find him?"

"Yes."

"Now?"

"Right now I want to see the polar bears." As we passed the carousel, Samm said we should ride it first.

"Aren't we too old?" I said.

"I'm not," she laughed. "Are you too old? Too embarrassed?"

"No. Maybe both. I don't know."

"How cute." Samm grabbed my hand and pulled me toward the line.

"Maybe we should borrow a kid?" I said.

"That's funny," she said, "and creepy. Mostly creepy."

"I see that now."

When they let us in, the little kids ran straight for the inside row of horses. That was where you sat if you wanted to try to grab the gold ring. Samm waited and then mounted a remaining outside horse and I got on one next to her.

"Are we allowed to reach for the ring?" I asked.

"We should never stop," she said.

"I'm thinking about the children."

"Because they're the future?"

"Because they're smaller than us," I said.

"I knew that," Samm said.

"Right. You made a joke." I needed to relax. She was funny which made her even cooler. "It was funny."

Some kid reached for the ring and missed and slipped off his ride before his parents could catch him. I couldn't remember what prize they gave you if you got the ring.

"That was less fun than I remember," Samm said as we left the carousel.

"Doing it with you is more fun than I remember, but the ride itself," I said, "less exciting."

"Growing up does seem to take the fun out of life."

"Wait," I said, stopping near the Bandshell. "Do you mean that?"

"Maybe."

"How did you determine that?" I asked.

"I don't know if I mean it. Mostly, I said it because it sounds like it's true at the moment. But it doesn't matter if I'm right because getting older isn't a choice."

"You make that sound so sad."

At the Bandshell, two guys and a girl were singing that Marvin Gaye song about the grapevine. They were having fun and they were good.

"Want to listen for a bit?" I said.

"Do you play?" she asked.

"No." I laughed. "Unless you count those three years of tenor sax in the junior high band."

"Why'd you stop?" she said.

"It wasn't an option. I sucked. And that was not just my opinion. It was a consensus. Teachers, the rest of the band, neighbors, my parents, little children. They all begged me to stop. What about you? You look like a musician."

"Really?" she said tilting her head. "What does a musician look like?"

I thought Samm was beautiful and I needed her to be a musician. "I can't describe it, but I know a musician when I see one."

"And you think I look like one?"

"Definitely," I said. She just stared at me. I made a note to never play poker with her. "I'm sticking with that," I added because her face remained unchanged.

"I play the cello," she finally said.

I swallowed fast and coughed. "So, I was right?" I put my hand out so she could give me some skin. Her hand was warm and soft.

"Lucky guess. And you don't believe in luck."

"No luck involved," I said. "Are you good?"

"I will be."

"I don't follow."

"When I think about the people I consider good, when I compare myself to musicians I admire, well I'm just beginning."

"Where do you go to school?" I said eyeing the pretzel cart near the benches.

"High School of Performing Arts."

"Really?" I said.

"Why would I lie?"

"I mean, it's impressive," I said, feeling a bit intimidated. "Let's get a couple of pretzels and listen to these guys."

We found a bench and I sat as close to Samm as I could without touching her.

"So Zach," Samm said. "If you're not good at music, what are you good at?"

"I don't know," I said. "I think I have few talents, but a shitload of interests"

"That's funny, but it's crap," she said. "Answer the question."

"I feel like I haven't been tested yet, haven't been in the position where what I did, what choice I made, meant anything or made any difference."

"Every choice makes a difference in your life."

"Sure," I said. "But I think the thing you're good at should mean something, should make a difference, should contribute. Like school, that's all about the future. Planning ahead. Waiting and putting off gratification. I mean, those are good things, they're fine qualities to have, but they come with a price, they come with a conscious ignoring of the present. Does that make sense?"

"Maybe," Samm said. "But if it's important to you, if it's something you love, doesn't that count? Doesn't the process count?"

"Are we talking about you and music now?"

"You're still avoiding the answer. You're Ali's brother, so I bet you're good at something. Probably a lot of things."

"That's mostly a compliment about Ali," I said. "Anyway, I'm good at math."

"But you're a little embarrassed to be good at it?"

"Maybe a little."

"Okay, but do you like math?" Samm asked. "Or do you like being good at it?"

"Both." Jonah was going to kill me because somehow I had managed to find a topic less interesting than the war. But Samm kept asking questions, so I told her how I was drawn to the logic, and that I loved that there was a right answer. but that there were usually several ways to arrive at that answer. I liked that numbers didn't have opinions. I liked that there was a mathematical field in which parallel lines could meet and that infinity plus one could exist. Numbers had never let me down. I told her that I thought it was cool that numbers were the same in any language, like a common language. Like music, I added.

"Just how easy does it come to you?" she asked. "Because I have to work at the cello. I'm thinking you were given a gift. I wasn't given a gift. I practice a lot. I mean, everyone who is good practices a lot. But, the gift for me is that I found something I love. But I am not gifted."

"I'm sure you're being modest."

"I wish I was. I've seen gifted," Samm said. "I mean they work as hard as I do, but their work is easier and their progress is smoother."

I told her that I worked at math, but it was rarely a mystery. Math had always made sense to me. Then I told Samm that I didn't like that math was used in the formula for napalm and nuclear bombs and missile trajectories. I said all that, and I also told her that that was why I was giving up math and not going to study it in college like I had planned and like everyone thought I would. Sure, I was always told it was a gift, but then wasn't it my choice what to do with my gift?

"That's just dumb," Samm said.

I had never enjoyed being called dumb as much as that moment.

She was so cute I hardly cared what she said to me.

"It's not up to you whether to use your gift and you're not very smart if you think otherwise."

"How is it not my choice?"

"Not using a gift is the same as quitting," she said. "What if Superman just quit trying to save the world because it doomed him to a lonely solitary life?"

"You like Superman?"

"He never gave up on people. But my point is that if you don't like that numbers are used for war, then do something about it. Like Superman would. Be the one to figure out how to use numbers to stop wars instead of starting wars."

"Sure, that sounds good in theory. But here's the thing. Life is not only what we make of it. It's also, and maybe mostly, what other people do to screw with your plans. We're too often at the mercy of the things other people do, things that intrude on our lives." At that moment I heard Jonah's voice in my head yelling at me to stop trying to depress Samm.

"What happened to you in your short life to come up with that?" Samm asked me.

Once again, I wondered if I had gone too far. "It's simply about numbers. The more people, the more chance for someone else's life to mess with yours."

"Tell me more about what you love about numbers," Samm said.

"I can do that," I said. "But only if I can put my arm around you." Samm slid closer to me and I put my arm around her and tried to remember the question.

"See, there are some advantages to getting older," she said.

"Like what?"

"Really? You can't think of anything?"

"This," I blurted out. "This. We can do this."

"I knew you'd get it," Samm said, tapping my chest. "Now, more about numbers."

"I always thought numbers would help me find the truth." I finally said.

"About what?"

"Everything."

"You think there's a truth about life? Or maybe you just hope there is."

"I deserve that," I said. "Tell me why you love music."

"There is so much of what we know that can't be explained in words or formulas."

"Things not seen."

"Precisely. Other ways of knowing. Sometimes it's in music or a painting or a photograph or a poem or a book. For me it's music and the cello, that's how I do music."

"For me," I said, "it's not so much that I thought I could use numbers to find the truth of life, it's that I thought they would be a guide of sorts."

"Why do you need a guide? Why can't you lead?"

"Because I have no idea where to go. And because I don't want to go alone."

"You're worried about being a prime number?"

"Yes."

"Just yes? You're not impressed that I know how to use prime numbers in a sentence?"

"Outstanding."

"Better."

"I live in my own head a lot," I said. "By myself."

"Follow me," Samm said as she jumped up and started running.

I caught up with her and took her hand and we walked the rest of the way to the zoo. As we watched the penguins do their thing, I leaned against Samm and kissed her. Her lips were delicious and her smell intoxicating. It all felt so easy and so natural.

"You can't write a formula for how I feel right now," I said.

"I think you should try," Samm said. "But this is one of those times where you should stop talking."

"Right." I kissed her again. For the first time in a long time, I wasn't trying to make sense of everything or anything. I wasn't wondering how I would know who was right if everyone was wrong. I didn't care about the sound of silence. And even though nothing made any more sense than it did before, right then, a moment had arrived.

After we left the polar bears, Samm wanted to get burgers at a diner she liked on 2nd Avenue. I had a joint and we smoked it on the way there.

"I love diners," I said.

"You're from New York. It's in your blood."

"So, I'm a cliché."

"Maybe. But that's our thing. New Yorkers love diners. I'm a New Yorker. So you're ok."

I followed Samm to a booth and while we waited on our burgers, she told me she was born at New York Presbyterian Hospital on the east side and grew up on the Upper West Side of Manhattan where she still lived. Went to PS 199 on West 70th before going to Julliard. She added that her parents, her grandparents, actually most of her family, had been born in Manhattan and had lived there ever since their great great great great grandparents arrived in New York from Ireland back in like 1820.

"My parents took me to Ireland, and it was great, but I don't feel Irish. I don't know where to say I'm from."

"You're from Manhattan?" I said.

"Sure," Samm said. "But, you know, where you're *from*."

"I'm from Queens." I was surprised that Samm found that funny.

"And you're also from Europe," she said. "You're like German and

Hungarian and Austrian and Israeli."

I liked that Samm found any of that interesting. "At what point are you simply from where you're from?"

"I'm not sure if that ever happens," she said. "Everyone is from somewhere else."

"But at some point, your geography is your destiny, not your history."

"I'm not sure I know what that means, or if it's even true."

"Neither am I."

The waitress brought our burgers and we traded talking for eating. I was looking out the window at the traffic and thinking of something to add that Samm would like. I wasn't sure how many details of my family's background to tell Samm. I was thinking of how to get us talking about something else, like music. Then I thought I saw Sunny across the street, waiting for the light to change.

"She's pretty," Samm said.

"What?" I said, looking back at Samm who was looking at Sunny. "I know her." I slid out of the booth and stood. "We need to ask her about David."

Samm didn't move.

"She's friends with these vets I met. They might know something. Maybe they could help you find David." I remained standing. "We need to hurry," I told Samm. "The light is changing."

The waitress came over and asked Samm if everything was okay.

"We're fine," Samm said. "Please sit down, Zach."

The waitress didn't move. I looked out the window. Sunny headed east and was quickly out of view. I sat back down and the waitress left.

"This place has great burgers, right?" Samm said. "Really good."

And it was a great burger. I didn't know what to make of Samm at that moment, so instead of asking what just happened, I took a big bite of my burger. "You need to come to Queens," I said as I chewed, "so I can take you to Sage Diner and you can meet Brucie."

"I'm scared to find him," Samm avoided my sideward invitation to Queens. "He's so different. I hardly recognize him."

I swallowed my food. "Do you think your brother would hurt you?"

"No," Samm said "Maybe. Not really. Not on purpose. But I'm scared to see him this way. I'm scared of who he's become."

"He listened to you that night. Maybe you could talk him into not going back."

"I can't talk him into anything. Not even our parents can. No one can except his army buddies."

I could tell she didn't want me to keep talking to her about David. I heard Jonah telling me to shut up.

"He knows he can stay, and he knows what going back will be like. His two tours were nine months each. And still, he wants to go back," Samm said. "I'm not sure his reasons are wrong. But the war is."

Before I could add anything else, Samm started talking about going to a movie. We finished eating in silence. The waitress brought the check and told Samm to say hi to David.

Outside, we walked to the river. We crossed over the FDR to the promenade and strolled holding hands. We stopped and sat on a bench in the shadow of the 59th Street Bridge. I put my arm around Samm because it was cooling off and because I liked doing it and mostly because she let me. Samm nestled against my shoulder, and it was good. I stroked her hair, and she looked up at me, and I kissed her. We stayed like that for some time, kissing and not noticing street lamps being lit up and apartment lights turning on. As we sat on a bench along the East River, we watched ferries and barges drift by. The traffic on the bridge created a stream of white and red lights moving in opposite directions. The sun was setting behind us as the city was illuminated around us as if it were waking up for the night ahead. And I was thinking how cool it was that I was sitting with a girl on a bench at the end of the summer in the city.

And wasn't she pretty?

"This is outstanding," I said.

"What?"

"Everything."

After a while, we got up and strolled back over to 2nd Avenue where we slipped into a club with an open mic for acoustic folk singers. We grabbed a table in a dark corner and ordered espressos. I was surprised by this woman who called herself Bex and sang a set of Tom Paxton covers. Her voice filled the room as she brought the audience along with her on an emotional vocal journey. A second espresso and four musicians later Samm needed to head home. Again, she didn't want me to take her, but this time I got her number, and we made plans to talk by phone and also to meet the following weekend.

After a long kiss that I didn't want to end, Samm headed west and I headed down the steps into the subway. I was on my way home from a date. I kind of wanted to say it out loud to everyone on the train. I was already thinking about the next time I would get to see her.

• • •

I found Jonah talking to a girl named Lu, and we hung out at the schoolyard for a while. When Lu had to go home, we left the schoolyard, too. When we got to Jonah's house, his dad was sitting alone in the living room. The only light in the house came from the TV. As usual, his dad didn't say anything to us, and we knew better than to disturb him. He may not have even been awake.

We closed Jonah's bedroom door and put Joe Cocker on the turntable and listened as he sang about how he was able to get by with nothing more than some help from his friends.

Jonah told me about Lu and how cool she was and how he was going to date her. I started to tell Jonah about walking around the city with Samm and how it didn't seem real and how I couldn't wait to see her again. But he missed most of what I was saying as he was fast asleep.

In the middle of the night, I got up to pee. I almost stepped on Jonah's sister, who was sitting on the bathroom floor.

"I got to go," I told her so she would let me pee in private. "Real bad," I added. Likely Wendy was wasted. When she didn't move, I turned on the light. That was when I saw that she was sitting in a pool of blood. She had a knitting needle in her right hand and she was still wearing my Hendrix t-shirt.

I ran back to the room and got Jonah up. He soared down the stairs and woke his parents. His mom nearly knocked me over in the hallway as she ran to the bathroom. His dad was right behind her.

"No one is calling an ambulance," Jonah's dad growled. "Don't need every neighbor knowing our business." He turned to me and Jonah. "You two help her outside. I'm going to pull the car out of the garage."

We helped Wendy into the back seat of their Oldsmobile with Jonah's mom next to her. Jonah went around and slid in on the other side of his sister. That left me sitting in the front seat with his dad. I tried to act like I was the navigator; like I was paying attention to the road in case Jonah's dad needed assistance. He did not. Besides, I had no idea where the hospital was. None of us said anything as we flew down empty streets and blew through red lights. And then I saw the ER sign. I was relieved to jump out of the car and help Jonah get Wendy out of the back while Jonah's mom ran inside to get help.

The nurses took Wendy right away even though the waiting room was crowded. Probably had to do with Wendy leaking blood on their floor. Jonah and I went to sit by ourselves so we could talk. Mostly he spoke. Mostly he complained about his father. Mostly nothing I hadn't heard before. I wondered if she was bleeding from her period and Jonah said I was sometimes really dumb for a smart guy.

After about a half-hour a doctor came out and called Jonah's family. We congregated in front of him as he updated us.

"She's lucky you found her when you did," he said to Jonah's dad.

"Zach found her," Jonah said. Nobody cared.

"As I was saying," the doctor continued, "she'll be all right, but she did do some damage to herself, and there's a possibility that she won't be able to have children. We won't know that until we see how she heals. But, it could have been a lot worse. A lot," he repeated. "We're sending her up to a room now and we'll monitor her overnight. You can go see her, but she's pretty groggy from the medication we gave her."

The doctor left, and Jonah's parents looked at us.

"She's going to be all right," his mother sighed.

"Appendicitis," his father said.

"What?" Jonah said.

"Her appendix burst."

"I know what happened," Jonah replied. "So does Zach."

I looked away. I wished Jonah hadn't brought my name into it.

"Your mother and I are going to get some coffee. Go sit with your sister, and we'll meet you in her room," he said.

"Go with Jonah," Jonah's mom said to me, squeezing my arm.

"If anyone asks," Jonah's dad said, "tell them appendicitis."

"Who's going to ask?" Jonah said.

"Don't get wise with me," his father said.

"I wasn't being wise," Jonah said. "I am not wise at all. It's four AM on a Sunday, and I just wanted to know who you thought might pass by so I could be prepared."

We found Wendy's room and Jonah pulled up a chair next to his sister. She looked different in her hospital gown. Someone had removed her earrings and her long brown hair, which was usually all over the place, was pulled back tight leaving her face exposed. She had a nice face. I'd known her my whole life, but I hadn't looked at her in a long time. She and Jonah did look alike. She was so still.

"Where's your friend," Wendy said to Jonah when she opened her eyes.

Jonah stood. "He's here."

"Come here, Zach," she said.

I went over and stood next to Jonah. Wendy motioned for me to lean in so she could whisper something. Instead she kissed my cheek. "Thanks," she said.

"I didn't do anything," I said. "I had to pee."

"Grandkids are on you now," Wendy told Jonah. "But not yet. Wear a fucking condom, okay?"

"You don't know that," Jonah said. "The doctor wasn't sure, which means you can't be sure."

"I am sure. And I'm glad. Kids are a pain. I'd probably get one just like me. This is a good thing. I can have sex and never have to worry about getting pregnant."

"Are you going to call Roger?" Jonah asked.

"Why?" Wendy asked.

"Tell him that you're here. Wouldn't he want to know?"

"All he wanted to know was if I was sure it was his."

Maybe Jonah's dad was right about Roger, I thought.

"Dad wants me to say you had appendicitis," Jonah said.

"You can imagine how little I give a shit what Dad wants or what you say."

"What are you going to tell people?" Jonah asked.

"To fuck off."

"That works."

Wendy tried to move, but you could tell she was in pain. "Hand me my cigarettes."

"You want to smoke now?" Jonah said.

"I'll get them myself." She tried to move again.

"I'll get them," I said.

Wendy lit a cigarette and inhaled deeply. "Want one?" She exhaled a thick stream of smoke. "No, you wouldn't." Her hands were shaking. "I wish I had a joint."

"Aren't you in enough trouble?" Jonah said.

"I'm not in trouble," Wendy said. "How is this trouble? And don't tell me you and Zach don't get high all the time. I smell it on your clothes."

Jonah's parents came back. His mom brought us hot chocolate. After a while, the nurse came in and suggested that we go home and let Wendy rest.

"I'm going to stay," Jonah told his dad.

I looked at Jonah and said, "I'll stay with him."

"Good," Jonah's mom said.

"Suit yourself," Jonah's dad said and left.

Jonah's mom kissed Wendy and then Jonah. She hugged me and thanked me and told Jonah to call if anything happened.

"You should get some rest," Jonah told Wendy after their parents left.

"I will," she said, closing her eyes. Wendy took a long drag from her cigarette, put it out in the bedside ashtray, and then whispered, "Whose did he think it was?" as she drifted off to sleep.

Jonah and I turned our chairs toward the window overlooking Fresh Meadows so we could watch the sun rise while Wendy slept.

"I used to think I was adopted," I said without looking at Jonah.

Jonah didn't say anything.

"I figured if my father couldn't walk," I continued, "then how could he have sex? How could he have kids?"

"You never talk about this," Jonah said.

"I know."

"Well, not with me."

"Not with anyone."

"Not even Ali?"

"Never."

"You look just like your dad," Jonah said. "So does Ali."

"Yeah,"

"So are you?"

I smacked Jonah's arm. He laughed.

"First of all, my mom would have told us."

"Hell, she would have told me."

"She would have told you for sure," I said.

"Did you ask her?"

"I went to the library to find out if he could have kids."

"When?"

"I don't know. I think I was ten."

"You are so fucking weird. Do you know that?"

"Yeah. And if I didn't, you tell me all the time."

"The library on 63rd?" Jonah asked.

"No, the one on Fifth Avenue."

"Why didn't you tell me? I would have gone with you."

"I don't know. I was scared what I might find out."

"What did you ask the librarian? Sexual habits of polio survivors?

"Something like that. At first she thought I was creepy. But once she figured out why I was interested she was all over me."

"Did you ever see your dad walk?" Jonah asked. "Like when you were little?"

With Wendy resting quietly behind us and with the darkness reluctantly giving way to light through the window in front of us, I told Jonah that the closest I ever came to seeing my father walk was on Saturday mornings when I helped strap him into braces. As he lay on the bed, I manipulated his body till the braces were under him. Then, I methodically secured the four straps around each leg, the two that held each knee and fastened the buckled band around his waist. Finally, I tied the laces on the black high-top leather shoes before I re-checked that the knee hinges were securely locked in place to prevent buckling. It's not like we ever unlocked them, but I re-checked anyway.

With all inspections complete, I spun my father's body around until his legs hung in the air over the side of the bed. At that point, I straddled his knees, and with outstretched arms grabbed hold of his hands and pulled him to sitting position. Then, with crutches tucked neatly underneath his arms, I walked backwards, pulling him into a standing pose, which always made me notice how tall a man he was. We shuffled across the three feet of floor that separated his bed and the bedroom wall. Once there we turned 180 degrees so my father could lean back and, supported by the wall and his crutches, stand vertical against the earth. While he defied gravity, I backed up into and sat on the edge of the bed.

Then I told Jonah about the time I sat in his chair. My mother saw me and came in and said she needed to take the chair to wipe it down. Later she told me that I must never sit in the chair again. She added that my father wouldn't tell me, but seeing me in his chair is an image he could not bear.

So, I always sat on the edge of his bed and tried to act casual, as if this were the kind of thing all fathers and sons did together. But I was ready to spring into action and catch him if he leaned too far, unable to counter the pull of gravity. That never happened, though. What did happen was my father would ask me questions about school and friends. But mostly he told me stories.

That was when I learned that immediately after he and his parents survived Vienna's night of shattered glass, the Jewish community gathered their youth and hastily shuttled them out of the city and out of the country to meet a ship that would take them to Palestine. When my father's boat arrived in Haifa, the teens were met at the port by members of the Irgun who handed each of them a tourist visa. Those with relatives in Palestine were shepherded into various vehicles and dispersed to predetermined meeting places throughout the city. Those with no one in the country, like my father, were taken to a youth camp on Mount Carmel.

• • •

During the days, my father learned Hebrew and performed chores around the camp while he waited for news of his parents' arrival. New campers arrived and others left as their families arrived. Many were relocated to one of the many kibbutzim forming to the north. At night, my father played chess or read and waited. Over two months passed before he heard confirmation that his parents were among a handful of Viennese Jews who did not survive the spontaneous mobs during the days that followed *Kristallnacht*.

My father listened to the news and remained standing still in that same spot for three hours. If he didn't move, then maybe his life would remain unchanged from the words he had just heard.

But he did move. Of course he moved because he was still alive. That much he knew. When the sun set my father returned to his bunk and packed his belongings. Without parents, he no longer belonged in a youth camp. Without parents he was no longer a child.

With a suitcase in each hand, my father walked down the mountain into Haifa and wove his way through the streets to the newspaper office. It was the middle of the night when he arrived and the offices were empty and the door was locked, so he sat down on the steps and he waited. In the morning, Chaim, the newspaper's editor, arrived for work, and found my father asleep.

"I arrived one season ago," my father said. "Right before the rains, while a dust storm rolled across this holy land. The newness of this ancient land, it's new to me," he told Chaim. "I've never felt like this before."

"It never goes away, that feeling," Chaim responded. "I was born here and I assure you that I too have felt that sense of wonder and those feelings, they never go away."

"I want to tell the world the story of this land," my father said. He grabbed his bags and followed Chaim inside and sat by his desk and would not leave until Chaim agreed to give him a job, any job. Chaim relented and let my father sort mail, answer phones, and help out where needed. Chaim even took him home and let him stay on his couch until my father could find a room of his own.

One day, my father answered a phone call, and instead of handing it off to a reporter, he asked the questions he had heard others ask. He took some notes and handed the message to Chaim. Without looking up, Chaim said, "Keep doing that."

A month later, Chaim did look up and handed the notes back to my father and said, "Okay."

"Okay what?"

"Okay, this one is yours. Go out and get this story. If it's good, I will print it with your name."

The story was easy, but his name gave him trouble. No way my father wanted his first, and possibly only, byline to be under his Austrian name. So he wrote the story, and then wrote his new Hebrew name, Abraham Hineni.

As soon as the paper was published, my father made his way directly to the courthouse to make his name change official. His co-workers didn't need to wait for the government papers to come back. They simply began calling him Hineni and Chaim continued assigning him stories.

One year later, on his eighteenth birthday, Chaim made it official. My father was given his own desk.

• • •

It had rained all day in the Holy Land, typical for December, when my father returned to Haifa. He had been gone for five days on an assignment that began with interviewing newly arrived Polish refugees at Kibbutz Ramat Rachel on the outskirts of Jerusalem. Chaim extended my father's trip when word came that the Knesset had left Tel Aviv and was going to hold its session in Jerusalem. Since my father was close by, Chaim told him to stay and cover the historic moment.

Stepping off the bus and into the rain, my father stretched, glad to be freed from the confines of the three hour ride. He walked the six blocks back to the newsroom and got to work at the desk he shared with Tamar, the theater critic. Satisfied with his story, he pulled the last page out of the typewriter. After carefully returning the carbon copy sheet to the top draw, he slipped his notes and his copy into the bottom drawer and jumped up. He grabbed his coat and dropped the article on his editor's desk.

"I'm done, Chaim," my father said, slipping on his coat. "I'll see you on Sunday." He began to make his way to the door.

"Abraham," Chaim said, "sit. Wait till I read it."

"It's good. It's always good. But mostly I've got a date tonight and I haven't changed clothes or bathed in three days. It wouldn't hurt you to go out on a date. Women like powerful men."

Chaim had been at the newspaper for close to thirty years, holding almost every position on his way to becoming editor-in-chief. He was the only editor my father had known.

"If I'm a powerful man, why can't I get you to sit?" Chaim said. "Who is it this time?" Chaim asked.

"Miriam."

"Really?" Chaim asked, still reading. "Again?"

"Why the surprise?"

"No surprise. Are you serious about her?"

"Possibly. I'm not sure yet."

"This is the fourth time she's cooking for you."

"Sixth."

"Is that a record for you?

"I don't keep count," my father said. "Yes."

"When a girl cooks you meals, Abe, and you continue to eat them, you're saying that you're serious.

"Maybe I'm saying that she's a seriously good cook?" my father smiled. "Maybe when we were back in Vienna it meant something," Abe continued. "Things are different here."

Chaim stopped reading and looked. "Abe, we've known each other, how long?"

"Ten years," my father said.

"Yes, ten years. And in all those years, how many times have I had to remind you that I was born right here in Haifa."

"Daily," my father laughed.

Chaim resumed reading. "Things are not so different anywhere," he added, looking up at my father.

"That is a pity then," my father said. "But, I am different and Miriam is different. We will make things different."

"Maybe." Chaim returned his attention to my father's article. "Outstanding work," he said when he was done. "Okay, get out of here. But I want details on Sunday."

"Then details you shall get."

It was still raining when my father left the newspaper building and began to run toward his apartment. He had always loved running in the rain. More than jumping over puddles and splashing through streams, he loved how everything smelled during a rain.

Back in Vienna, he had been a runner for his upper-secondary school. During his second year, he won the city championship in the steeplechase. The following year he was no longer allowed to compete or attend school.

As my father turned onto Jacobi Street, his legs felt strong and responsive. He leaped over benches, maneuvered around pedestrians, avoided cars and buses and mopeds. The run was washing away the long hours of meetings and travel and arguments over rules and procedures. He started thinking about the next day's soccer game. That Saturday pick-up game had become a regular for all the neighborhood's European immigrants – observant and secular. Soccer was their common language. Swear words happened in mother tongues, German, Polish, Hungarian, French, Hebrew, Arabic – and were easy to identify if not translate. My father was on a mission to learn them all.

He taught me a few. My favorites were "fuck" in Polish, *pierdolic*. And "for fucks sake" in Hungarian, *a kurva eletbe*. I thought it would be fun to say them at the park where no one spoke those languages. But just like in my father's soccer games, everyone knew I was swearing and I almost got my ass kicked. And then a couple of kids asked me to teach them.

But if you asked any of the players at the Saturday pick-up games if they thought that among their mates were future leaders of the State of Israel, they all would have laughed and each would have responded, yes, of course, and pointed to themselves. Not everyone made it, but the numbers show that their confidence was not arrogance: three prime ministers, two presidents, four mayors, two generals, and at least seven members of parliament. And that didn't include leaders outside the government.

Wet and refreshed from his run, my father arrived home and was greeted by Shlomo and Liora, his married orthodox roommates. They were preparing for their Shabbat dinner and invited my father to join them. He explained about his dinner with Miriam and started a bath.

"You should invite Miriam here for a Shabbat dinner," Shlomo said through the bathroom door.

"She has as little interest in religious ritual as I do," Abe said. "Possibly less."

"That's not likely," Liora chimed in.

"Ask her anyway," Shlomo said. "It's just food."

"Appreciate the offer, but it's unlikely that I will invite her."

"Why?" Shlomo asked.

"Because I'd like to keep seeing her."

When he arrived at Miriam's apartment, my father was greeted by her disarming smile and the smell of her lamb stew. Miriam, a blonde-haired sabra and Haifa native, worked as a high school history teacher and was writing a book on the history of Mount Carmel.

After dinner, they lit cigarettes and lay on the couch.

"It's strange," he said. "I don't feel right. I can't taste much this evening. Not even this cigarette."

Miriam touched my father's forehead and suggested they take his temperature. When the thermometer read one hundred and two, they decided to skip the movie and my father headed back home.

Shlomo and Liora were reading and quite surprised to see my father return home so early. He explained that he had caught his usual winter cold.

"I'll be better in the morning," he told them and went to bed.

The next morning, after sweating all night, he was surprised that his temperature had not fallen at all. Shlomo and Liora stayed home from shul despite my father's protests. After lunch, Liora walked down the block to fetch the doctor who seemed annoyed when he diagnosed it as just a cold and gave my father some pink pills to reduce the fever. On Sunday morning, fever still unbroken, my father called Chaim and told him he wouldn't be coming in. When Shlomo and Liora left for work they left my father on the couch so he could be near the phone.

Later, my father needed every bit of his strength to walk to the bathroom. He would forever recall that moment, standing unsteadily in front of the toilet and peeing. It was the last time he stood on his own strength.

When they returned home from work, Shlomo and Liora were surprised to find my father on the couch. And a little concerned. Liora made him some tea while Shlomo brought the daily paper over and sat with him and read the news.

"Someday," my father said, "we are going to have to figure out how to co-exist with the Arabs. It's not a matter of justice or ethics – well it is that too," he added – "but really, it's a matter of practicality. If we don't find a way to co-exist, we, both Jews and Arabs will spend most of our resources, and spill much of our blood, fighting each other. And the world will, once again, have an excuse to hate Jews."

"Abe," Shlomo said, "you know the world never needs a reason or even looks for an excuse to hate Jews. That's why Israel needs to be more than a safe place for Jews and why it needs to be a Jewish state."

"I fear we've made Israel less safe for Jews by handing over so much power to the rabbis."

"But Abe, it's observant Jews who are the future of the Jewish people."

While my father usually enjoyed debating Shlomo and often initiated these discussions, he felt too weak to continue.

"Have some tea," Liora said, handing my father a cup.

"I think I'd like to go to bed," my father said. "Can you help me?"

The next morning, Shlomo called the newspaper to say my father would miss another day. Chaim told him to leave the door open as he was on his way over.

"You haven't missed ten minutes in ten years," Chaim said when my father laughed at his concern. Chaim sat for a few minutes without removing his overcoat before suddenly standing up and heading out. He shouted to my father to stay put.

"Where would I go?" my father called back.

But it was too late. Chaim was already running to the office of his friend, Dr. Meyer.

"Chaim," Dr. Meyer told him, "I'm a heart specialist."

Still, Chaim insisted he follow him back to see his friend. "I don't care if you're a heart doctor or a horse doctor," Chaim said, handing Dr. Meyer his coat. "I know you and I need you to come with me immediately."

Together, on foot, they hurried through the streets of Haifa. Without even the briefest of greetings, Dr. Meyer started to examine my father. First, he looked into his eyes. Then he ran a pin down the middle of his belly and along the soles of his feet. My father searched the doctor's eyes for a trace of reaction, a hint at a diagnosis, but found no clues. Dr. Meyer lifted my father's eyelids and peered into his pupils with a flashlight. By then, my father understood that the doctor was genuinely concerned.

Abruptly, Dr. Meyer stood and took Chaim into the living room. My father watched through the open door, but was unable to hear what Dr. Meyer was telling Chaim. My father watched as Dr. Meyer lifted the receiver and made a phone call. After replacing the receiver he turned and quickly left the apartment.

Chaim returned to my father's bedside, overcoat still on.

"Should I be worried?"

"You shouldn't be worried."

"What does he think it is?" my father asked.

He'd never seen that look on Chaim's face, but it needed no explanation.

Chaim sat down on the bed. "Dr. Meyer isn't sure what you have, but he wants you at the hospital where they can run some tests."

"What kind of tests?" my father asked.

"He didn't say."

"Did he say anything?" my father asked.

"He said to get you to the hospital right away."

"Is that it?" my father asked.

As he looked closer into Chaim's eyes, he knew it was not good, and that there were things he was not being told. He had never seen fear in Chaim. Not when armed British entered the newspaper office claiming to be looking for illegal immigrants after a particularly nasty editorial. And not when Tamar, the theater critic, went into labor right at press time, and Chaim had to help deliver her child while they waited for the ambulance.

"That's it," Chaim said.

"But you are worried."

"I always worry," Chaim laughed.

My father, who was born at his parent's home in Vienna, had never been to a hospital. Ever. Had never even visited anyone in a hospital. While he lay immobile in his bed, deciding that he would not go to the hospital, two large men entered the apartment and his room and, with Chaim watching, they lifted him onto a stretcher and carried him down the stairs to the waiting ambulance. On the drive through the familiar streets of Haifa, my father gathered what strength he could to let Chaim know he would fight. That he would will his body to do more than it was supposed to.

Of course, he would think that. My father had, after all, survived *Kristallnacht*, survived the trip out of Europe, the voyage across the sea, the coming ashore undetected by the British, the trek into Haifa, the random bombings, the occasional gunfire, the war of independence. There was no reason for him to be done in by an invisible bug, the smallest of living cells.

No matter how weak he felt, no matter how tired he was, he was not going to give in. He owed that much to his parents, to Chaim, to himself. He had seen men and women let themselves die. He had seen friends give up hope and wither away. He was not going to let that happen. He was young and he was not done.

There were great things to accomplish and he had hardly begun to do his part. He had always been certain that he would have a role. "We made it to the precipice," he told Chaim. "We're a nation, and I'm not going away without taking that leap forward," he told Chaim as he drifted off.

The Government Hospital in Haifa was a large stone building that sat on the Mediterranean Sea. By the time he was admitted and placed in a room, he was unconscious. On the second day, Dr. Meyer had his suspicions confirmed.

My father had polio.

That he would never walk again, the doctors were certain. That he would live, they were less certain.

On the third day, as my father slept, there was an explosion at the newspaper building killing all seventeen people in the office at the time. Had my father not been near death, and if Chaim had not been sleeping by his near-death bedside, both would have been killed.

When his fever finally broke, my father opened his eyes and saw Chaim asleep in the chair by the open window overlooking the sea. As his senses returned, he heard the sound of the waves against the shore and inhaled the salty breeze. But then he tried to stir and found his muscles did not respond. He wiggled his fingers and then his toes and then managed to wiggle his arms and his legs. And then his mind raced forward without answers about a body that had lost almost all of its capabilities. He took a deep breath. "Sleepyhead," he called to Chaim.

"You've decided to join us again," Chaim said, sitting up quickly, smiling.

"I must have fallen asleep in the ambulance, my father said. I see they gave me a nice room," he laughed, trying to act normal.

"That was four days ago, Abe. You fell asleep four days ago."

"Four days?"

"Yes." Chaim stood next to the bed.

"And you've been here for four days?

"Yes."

"You weren't sure I would wake up?"

"I knew you would," Chaim said as he went to find the doctor.

"But the doctors, they were less sure?" my father called after him.

Chaim returned, followed by several doctors. They probed and poked and whispered and conferred. This was an unusual case. Only the second one they had seen. In the end, orders were given to have my father transferred to the Hadassah Hospital in Jerusalem where he would receive rehab with the goal of regaining enough strength to make the journey to New York where polio treatment was more advanced.

Chaim expressed disappointment that the transfer to Jerusalem would make visiting more difficult, especially now that he had to reconstruct the newspaper operation, but he would come on his days off.

"Don't worry," my father told Chaim. "I've always wanted to live in Jerusalem. Now I get to."

In Jerusalem, my father's hospital room provided him with a view that looked out over the ancient walls of the city. The evening nurse, Hannah, sat by his bedside and spooned soft foods into his mouth.

On the third night, my father took a deep breath and remembered who he was. As he exhaled, he became a reporter again. He decided that he would no longer be reduced to just another patient lying on his back being spoon fed by a nurse. He asked Hannah questions about her life, her work, her family as she nourished him. My father quickly dispensed with the standard biographical material. He then moved on to questions about news of the State of Israel. He asked her about new movies and theater openings and he asked her about her life.

Hannah worked nights because she liked the stillness, she had told him. After her rounds, if the shift was quiet with no duties pressing, she wheeled my father out onto the roof garden of the hospital. Up on the roof, high above the Jerusalem gates, they shared cigarettes and looked out over the ancient city and the surrounding hills. My father wanted to know everything about Hannah's youth in this holy city. Every so often, Hannah leaned over to remove the cigarette from his mouth to tap the ashes off and then return it. With his strength returning, Abe sang to her. He sang songs in his native Austrian and his adopted Hebrew. He dictated poems, and Hannah wrote them down, and then he read them to her. By the time he was ready to be sent off to New York, my father had convinced Hannah to stop complaining about the incompetent doctors and become one.

"You want me to become an incompetent doctor?" she asked.

"That is totally up to you," he said. "But in every situation, there are always at least two possibilities. And for each of those possibilities," he continued, "there were two more. And so on, so that you always have at least two choices. So you can try to be a great doctor or an incompetent doctor. In the end, he told her, you are what you settle for."

"And what are your possibilities?" she asked.

"I have polio, of course," he told her. "But polio is not my only possibility. It's not the end for me. It's another beginning. A new adventure."

And then, a decade after my father, Abraham Hineni, stepped off the boat and onto the Haifa beach, two years after the United Nations haphazardly partitioned British-ruled Palestine, and a year after a motley band of Jews declared Israel a nation state, he returned to the same sea. But leaving required assistance. Chaim, helped by two orderlies, carried him onto the ship that would take him away from the adopted land he had come to love. The polio that had the possibility of killing him, chose instead to exile him.

Chaim, my father, and Hannah didn't say it, but they all understood that my father would not be returning to Israel any time soon. If at all.

A week later, after passing through Ellis Island, my father was admitted to the Center for Joint Diseases in Manhattan where he was fitted with a full body cast to stabilize his muscles, unaware that this latest innovative care and treatment was the worst of all possible therapies. This newest treatment was administered with well-intentioned guessing by a dedicated staff who were over-matched by this tiny virus.

Around the same time, the Center for Joint Diseases was receiving daily admits of Israeli soldiers flown to New York to receive treatment for severe battle wounds. My father's doctors thought the camaraderie would be a benefit to him and they had the nurses move his bed to the floor with his countrymen.

He was transferred from the second floor to the fourth floor where his bed was slipped in next to Yaakov, who was about the same age as my father and who had the misfortune of stepping on a land mine and losing both his legs. Yaakov and my father quickly became close friends and chess rivals. Yaakov was capable of lighting their cigarettes and moving the pieces on the chess board. Their epic games quickly attracted an audience who, as chess players themselves, understood that these two players were not locked in any ordinary game.

And then one day, Leah appeared. She had come from Jerusalem to stay with her aunt, but had shortly received news that her childhood friend, Yaakov, was in a hospital in New York. She was anxious to find him and visit.

Leah came by most evenings, stopping at each bedside, speaking with every Israeli on the floor. The nurses were glad to have her spend a few moments talking to them in Hebrew. It was clearly medicinal. For those that needed the help, she wrote letters home, lit cigarettes, read them their mail. Before leaving for the night, Leah gathered the patients around her and read the day old Israeli newspaper she'd picked up at the newsstand on her way over – everyone listened, and everyone had a comment. Often, more than one comment.

When Yaakov returned to Israel with his new replacement legs, Leah continued to visit her guys. By then, my father was out of his cast and needed less help. But helping was never why Leah stopped by his bed, nor was it why she returned often and stayed longer than she sat by any other patient – a fact pointed out by the other patients as soon Leah went home for the evening.

Leah didn't understand how my father was able to make her feel like he was taking care of her. And she was not one who needed taking care of.

He makes me feel cherished, she wrote Yaakov. *And he makes me laugh. Freely laugh.*

She was not asking, nor was Yaakov answering, when he wrote Leah back to say that he was certain that Abe was indeed a good man, a special man. *He's one of us,* he told her. *We are brothers,* Yaakov added.

One year after my father was released from The Center for Joint Diseases, two years after he had passed through Ellis Island, he and Leah were married. Their friends and guests were impressed that they emptied their small, ground floor, Brooklyn apartment of its furniture to make room for the party. In truth, however, they did not yet, at the time of their wedding, have any furniture besides a bed. Though, of course, my father already had a chair.

Two months later, when my father began his desk job in the Israeli government's Manhattan office, he and my mother had purchased a couch. At work, it made no difference that Abe was unable to stand or make use of a chair. It only mattered that he was smart and fearless. In the government offices, he belonged. He was no longer in medical exile. Instead, he was an Israeli living abroad.

• • •

And that is how I became the progeny of refugees with thick accents who passed on their heritage of the gloom of war and the promise of peace. They exhibited the kind of self-assurance that comes from having survived and the mistrust of having had to.

I listened to their stories about each of the many who didn't make it. I learned Europe's geography by its death camps and its death tolls. I could place thumbtacks on a map where the ovens and the gas chambers had been. I could name the ghettos and I knew where people and things now gone had once been.

SURREALISTIC PILLOW

The impossible happened. Or maybe it was the improbable. The Mets clinched the National League East and were headed to the playoffs for the first time in team history. The first playoff game was going to be played on Saturday which was also my birthday. As we walked to school that Friday, we met up with Lu by the overpass on 67th Street. She and Jonah had been dating since that night they met in the schoolyard. Her family had moved to Queens from Nashville, and she was different and funny and had this appealing accent. She enjoyed Jonah's accent, too, and was always finding a way to get him to say "water."

When we reached Queens Boulevard, Tony and Mel were waiting.

"Is he giving you today's Vietnam score?" Tony asked.

"Of course," Jonah said.

"Your mom and I were hoping it was just a phase," Tony told me.

"We were sure you'd grow out of it by now," Mel added. "Well, less sure, more hoping."

"Thirty-seven more today," I said, reading from the tiny notebook I had taken to carrying around with me.

Jonah put his hand over the page. He had never done that before. "Not today," Jonah said. "Today, we ignore."

"The war isn't on pause today?" I said.

"Put the damn book away," Jonah said. "No death tolls. No war reports. No politics. It's all baseball, all the time."

"Okay." I slipped the book back into my pocket. "But I'm still writing the numbers in my book."

"I need you to focus,"Jonah said. "Be baseball, or be nothing." He made me promise to shut everything down for the rest of the playoffs.

"It's cool that you care," Mel said, "but you need to take a break sometimes. You can't care that much every second. It's not healthy. Plus, Tony has a surprise."

"I hate surprises," I said.

"Then you will hate this," Mel said.

"Okay. Listen up. I have an announcement," Tony said as we turned onto 108th Street. He stopped walking and so did we. He put his hand on my shoulder. "A proclamation, actually," he added.

"Then proclaim you shall," I said.

"I proclaim that we are having a birthday party in your honor on Saturday night," Tony said.

"Awesome," Jonah said.

"I don't do birthdays," I said.

"We don't care," Tony said.

"We *really* don't," Mel added.

"My parents are going away, and we're throwing a party in your honor. It will be, in your words, *outstanding*."

"You must invite Samm," Lu said.

"It's time we met her," Mel said.

"But she doesn't know it's my birthday."

"So tell her," Jonah said.

"Seriously, Zach," Lu said, "Stop whining."

Later that day, Tony came to my math class and ceremoniously removed a copy of the new Blind Faith album from a plain brown paper bag and presented it to me. The one with a naked girl on the cover. That was his way of making sure Lisa, my math partner, knew it was my birthday. But mostly, I think he enjoyed seeing me squirm while holding the picture of the girl in class.

"You could have given me this on the way to school," I said.

"And miss this moment?"

"Exactly," I said.

"Invite her to your party," Tony said as he left. I quickly slipped the album into my desk.

"Not so fast," Lisa said, reaching in and removing the album from my desk. She lifted it and examined the cover. "Is she your type?" she laughed, pointing at the girl on the album. She didn't wait for me to answer. "She's naked, that makes her every guy's type. But you do know, she's only eleven years old, right?"

I was hoping she'd put it away before Mr. Steel saw it and made a big deal of it.

"Wait," Lisa said, "I get it."

"Get what?" I said.

"It's a metaphor," she said. "Mets fans need blind faith."

"Yeah, that's it," I wasn't going to tell her that Tony didn't care about baseball.

"So how old are you, Zach?"

"I'll be fourteen tomorrow."

"You're kidding?" she said. "Fourteen," she said it like she had just figured out the solution to a problem. "You're in the same class as me and you're fourteen, and I'm eighteen."

She returned the album to me which I quickly slipped into my desk.

"What's it like being the youngest kid in AP Calc?" Lisa asked me. "you're probably the youngest kid in every class."

"Possibly," I said.

"I bet you don't think it's cool. I mean, it's a lot easier being the youngest girl," she said. "But it's going to be cool when you get out of here, out of high school, you'll see."

Lisa was right about one thing. Being the youngest kid in class stopped being cool the moment girls realized they liked older guys.

"Tell me about the party," Lisa said.

• • •

After school, I couldn't wait to call Samm and invite her to Tony's. She and I had been hanging out a bunch. Just the two of us. Really, anytime I could get to Manhattan, I did. On Saturdays, I'd meet Samm and go with her to Washington Square where she played her cello. But she didn't play for the donations, though she did collect quite a bit of loose change. She said playing like that in public helped her stay focused on the music and not what was going on all around her.

I would meet her at the West 4th Street subway and we'd walk to the park where she picked her spot to set up and play. The first time, I kind of felt like a bodyguard, keeping an eye on her cello case with the money. But I wasn't. Samm had been doing this on her own before she met me. So I was only there to watch and listen. It was indeed something to see. With her cello comfortably between her legs, she rested its scroll against her cheek as if inviting the instrument to be part of her.

Mostly, Samm played the classics. She taught me names like Dvorak and Schubert and Bach. But every so often she broke out a Dylan or a Led Zeppelin cover and that brought the crowd and the coins. I don't know if it was because they recognized a true musician in a park with too many posers, or if they liked hearing a classical instrument being used to produce some rock and roll. Like the way everyone loves a convert or a prodigal son.

When Samm was finished playing, Freddie, a homeless guy she knew by name, came over.

She had met Freddie the first time she played at the park. He had come up to her right after she'd finished playing Bach's Suite No. 1 and started talking to her. At first, she didn't listen because she was thinking about her next piece, and, frankly, because of the way he looked and smelled. He wandered away, but later that night, while she was packing up, Freddie came over again and offered some feedback about the cello and the Suite, and Samm understood quickly that he knew more than she did about both.

The next time she played at the park, Samm left the Suite for last and watched as Freddie, eyes closed, seemed to accompany her by moving an imaginary bow across an imaginary cello while his fingers moved precisely up and down imaginary strings. Freddie came over and talked cello with her as she packed up, and Samm offered him the money she had collected in her case.

Freddie took it, but then he made Samm take some of it back. "You don't live around here," he insisted. "You'll need it to get back home," he added.

From then on, Samm divided the cello money with Freddie as if they were in it together.

Sam told me that Suite No. 1 connected Freddie to his old life. In that life, Freddie was married and lived up in Washington Heights. His wife taught second grade in Chelsea and Freddie gave music lessons – any stringed instrument – to kids in the neighborhood. On weekends and occasional weeknights, Freddie played stand-up bass in a couple of jazz bands and electric bass in a highly sought after wedding band. But cello was his first instrument and his true love.

When he got drafted and sent to Korea, Freddie left behind his wife and their six-month-old daughter. In Korea, he decided that killing was better than being killed. And, it turned out he was good at it. After his initial obligation, he volunteered for a second 12-month combat tour. He survived and returned home to a wife who didn't recognize him and a two-year-old daughter who didn't know him.

There were lingering issues from having been in combat. At first, it was just the occasional waking up in a sweaty flashback. That seemed normal, and Freddie and his wife were confident it would pass. It got worse. Soon flashbacks were triggered by smells or street noises and they increased in frequency and severity and caused Freddie to leave the apartment less often. Music seemed to calm him down and his lessons and performances were unaffected. But getting to his gigs sometimes proved challenging, and it wasn't unusual for him to show up late which caused the bands to call him less.

And then one night his daughter's crying sent him into a rage, and he frightened both his wife and his little girl. A week later, he started choking his wife in the middle of the night and only stopped when she grabbed the nearby lamp and hit him on his head. That burden and the fear became too much, and his wife left that night with their daughter just one week before the baby girl's third birthday. She was sorry, his wife said as Freddie sat on the floor rocking himself and crying. He did not argue. He did not talk. He was as frightened as she was that he might hurt them.

When Freddie missed his second month's rent, the super knocked on his door and told him if he didn't pay up soon, the landlord was going to evict him. Freddie stood in the doorway and listened and didn't say anything. When the super was done talking, Freddie walked out of the apartment, past the super, and out of the building. He had been living on the streets ever since.

The first time I listened to Samm play in the park I didn't even notice Freddie until he came over after she was done with her set. He just started talking to Samm without any intro. He looked a bit dangerous or maybe it was just that his clothes were torn and dirty, but when I got close, it was clear that Samm liked talking to him and she introduced us. It took a few times of being there with Samm before Freddie spoke to me.

"Are you a friend of Samm?" he asked me.

"I am."

"Do you play?"

"Play?"

"Cello. Do you play cello?"

"No, I don't play."

"Do you know that Samm plays magnificently? Are you able to appreciate how good she is?" He sounded annoyed with me.

"I think so," I said.

"I doubt that. Most people can't."

"I like listening to her play," I said.

"Good," he said. "That's a start."

I was glad I finally gave Freddie an answer he liked.

"Listening," he continued, "*really* listening, is good. Try to hear what she is making the cello say. This is called Suite No. 1. It's not particularly challenging. Not like Barber. Most cellists perform it. It's not that difficult, so it has become well-known. But Samm, she draws its soul out as she draws her bow back and forth across those four strings. She gives the Suite the life and power Bach imagined when he wrote it. That's the difficult part. That's what makes her special. Do you get that?"

The question was clearly an accusation.

Freddy wasn't trying to teach me anything. I wasn't even sure he cared if I was listening to him. But then he turned and looked right at me. I had nothing to say in my defense.

"Samm breathes music. She *breathes* music." He paused as if to make sure I understood him. "It's a rare gift," he said, softly. He turned and looked at Samm and smiled and repeated, "It's a rare gift."

And then he stopped talking.

When the music stopped Freddie went to Samm to help her pack. I stayed back as Samm divided the evening's earnings.

Without saying goodbye, Freddie turned and walked away.

When we left Washington Square we strolled along McDougal toward Dante's where we ordered black coffees and toast with olive oil.

It was Samm's favorite cafe, and it only took one visit for it to become mine as well. I felt like we were in a foreign country, traveling incognito. Or Samm was a musician on tour and I was her roadie. Or maybe we were on the run and the cello was our suitcase in disguise as we made our way out of the country and across the sea. I imagined the streets of Paris or London or Rome littered with cafes like Dante's. Yes, we had the Stage, and my favorite waiter, Brucie, back in Queens, but Dante's cafe was something else, with its fabulous coffee, intimate tables surrounded by intense conversations in numerous languages and accents while wait staff stealthily delivered exotic food and strikingly named drinks.

Time stood still in Dante's. Not like the magical way baseball time stands still, but in the way that lets us sit without regard to purpose, without the need to accomplish. We could just sit. And no one seemed to care what we did or didn't do. It allowed our minds to wander and meander and collide and conspire. Our thoughts exploded with the irrational, the foolishness, the madness. Or, maybe it was just that we were hyped up on espressos. Samm always used the last of her cello money to leave a big tip for the waitress.

• • •

Jonah and I watched the Mets win a playoff game on my birthday, and later I went with him to pick up Lu, and the three of us went to meet Samm at the subway and bring her to Tony's.

Inside Tony's lobby, I pushed 6C and someone buzzed us in. We rode the elevator up and entered an already crowded apartment. As I surveyed the room I was blindsided by Tony who wrapped me in one of his patented bear hugs.

"You must be Samm," Tony said and didn't wait for an answer before hugging her. "I'm Tony," he added, releasing Samm and leading us into the living room where he introduced Samm to Mel.

Tony took a seat next to Mel and, like those old time cigar rollers, he went into joint production, using weed that was being collected in a large bowl on the coffee table.

Samm and I shared a big cushy chair, and Mel lit a joint which she passed to Samm. Someone brought up the topic of teachers and someone else said Ms. Parker, my English teacher, was the sexiest teacher in the school.

“And she knows she’s beautiful,” Angela said. When she spoke, her huge silver cross bounced back and forth between her breasts.

I wasn’t sure what she meant by that. I figured all the pretty girls knew how pretty they were. I assumed Samm knew. Clearly Angela knew.

“All the girls want to dress like Ms. Parker,” Mel continued. “And all the guys want to undress her.”

“To be fair,” Tony said, “we want to undress every girl.”

Mel threw her arms around Tony's neck and kissed him.

I lifted the bowl of weed and examined it.

“Easy there, Zach,” Tony laughed. “Don't do anything rash.” It was Tony’s idea to have everyone bring some pot and toss it in the bowl to share.

”Your pot bowl rule is outstanding. It’s like that Jesus fish story,” I said.

“It is,” Samm said.

“What do you know about Jesus?” Amy Black asked. I hadn’t noticed her sitting on the floor.

“Same as everyone else,” I said apologetically. “I read the New Testament.”

“My man Zach knows shit about everything,” Tony said. He grabbed a pile of joints and handed them to this guy Turtle. “Start lighting these and passing them around.”

“So, you’re kind of religious?” Amy asked me.

"Not at all religious," I said. "And I don't care to be. I just like the stories."

"Is that why you read it?" Amy said. "For the stories?"

"I was curious why the sequel was so popular."

"That's funny," Angela said as Samm passed her a joint. "'The sequel.' That's funny," she repeated and laughed.

"I saw you get Bar Mitzvah," Amy said to me.

"You did?"

"What's a Bar Mitzvah?" Angela asked.

"It's Jewish communion," Tony said. "It's when little Jewish boys become little Jewish men."

"So you're a man?" Angela smiled at me.

"According to my people," I said, "and Tony."

"That's so cool," Angela said. "And you're a Jew?"

"I'm Jewish on my parents' side," I said.

"I don't know many Jews," Angela said, though I couldn't tell if she was saying it to me. "I'm Catholic." She pulled her cross out from between her breasts as proof. As if I hadn't noticed it yet. "What's it like being Jewish?"

That caught me off guard. "I'm not sure what that means," I said.

"Like in my house, it's all about the Pope. Everything we do is judged by the Church. Do you guys have a Pope?"

"Some rabbis have more status, but there's nothing like a Pope," I said. "And my family is not religious, anyway."

"But you're still Jewish?" Angela asked.

"Yeah," I said.

"Which means you killed Jesus," she laughed.

"You do realize that I wasn't there?"

"Doesn't matter. My family would still hold you personally responsible."

"Maybe I shouldn't visit," I said

"My parents have that effect," Angela laughed.

"Don't forget that Joseph and Mary were Jewish," I said. "Which made Jesus Jewish too."

"Are you Jewish?" Angela asked Samm.

"I am not."

"And your parents are okay with you dating a Jew?" Angela asked.

"Well, they haven't met Zach, but yeah."

"That's cool," Angela said.

"What did you think?" Amy asked me.

"About my Bar Mitzvah?" I was confused.

"About the sequel," Amy said.

"I liked the parts when Jesus speaks. Like Jesus was as a revolutionary – a socialist. The way Moses was a freedom fighter. He might have been a Freedom Rider. And John the Baptist was a loner, an outsider, rejected by his peers. I think the Old Testament has better stories. Like Adam and Eve. Were they siblings who had kids? There's all kinds of incest and gay sex and rivalry and betrayal. Brothers don't fare well. And Jews even have books of stories about the stories called *midrash.*

"The parables are pretty good. I liked the riddles, too. But then, after the Gospels, after they kill off the main character, the story gets weird quickly. Like all those letters. And Revelations. That shit is some serious drug-induced writing."

"What about coming back from the dead?" Amy said. "You didn't like that? We don't have that."

I like that Amy said we. "That's confusing 'cause it's only in one of the Gospels. The whole plot relies on Jesus coming back from the dead, right? But only Matthew mentions it. Without the rising, there's not much to the story. But the other three guys never bothered to mention it."

"I'm a recovering Catholic," Tony said. I think he was trying to save me. "Served a six-year sentence at Our Lady of Perpetual Bullshit. That's why I smoke so much pot. It's part of my twelve joint program."

"It's every step of the program," Mel said.

"I'll smoke to that," Tony said.

"You don't think a virgin birth raises questions?" Amy asked me.

"Funny," Samm said, "that immaculate conception is where people get tripped up. If I were Joseph," she said, "it would raise a lot of questions. But if you believe in a god that created the world and everything else in six days, or that Moses parted the Red Sea, or that Jesus rose from the dead, well then, isn't a virgin birth almost like a cheap parlor trick."

I was so proud to be with Samm at that moment?

"That is hilarious." Angela laughed and her cross laughed with her.

"That is some wise shit, Samm," Mel said. "Or maybe we're just very high."

"Why can't it be both," Tony said.

"You have to wonder," Samm continued. "What kind of god would put Joseph through all that? Mary was his wife for god's sake. Isn't that one of the commandments? Not cool to get another man's wife pregnant. Did he commit adultery with Mary? Didn't he covet another man's woman?"

Mel laughed. "First god takes over her body and she has to give birth to his kid, and then he wants her to raise the kid without his help or even any child support, and then the kid, he brings a crowd everywhere he goes and everyone wants to come over his house all the time. And the disciples, they can't seem to do shit on their own without Jesus holding their hand. So they're useless. That means Mary got stuck feeding everyone and then staying behind and cleaning up the place while Jesus and his boys wander about giving speeches and dishing out miracles. The least god could have done was give Jesus some power to, you know, snap his fingers and clean up after himself?"

We were all hysterical at this point, until Amy added, "The thing I always found sad about Mary, is that she watched her son die. That is so wrong. God did that to her, too. Uncool."

We stopped laughing and no one said anything.

"To Mary," Mel said, breaking the silence.

"To Mary," we all responded.

Amy asked me about the fish story. She had never given me attention before. Was it because I was with Samm? I noticed that she had a Chai necklace. Was it there before? Did she pull it out because she saw Angela's cross? I was torn between dueling medallions. A dangerous place to be while sitting next to Samm.

"This one time Jesus was out in the wilderness with a large crowd," I said. "The disciples came to Jesus all worried that there wasn't enough food for everyone and the crowd was getting nervous."

"Bunch of whiners," Angela laughed.

"Jesus told them to be cool. He removed the few loaves of bread and pieces of fish that Mary had packed for him and the boys and put them in a basket and went into the crowd and told them to help themselves and then pass the rest for others to share. Suddenly, everyone was adding to the basket and soon there was enough food for everyone. So, either Jesus fed five thousand people with a few loaves of bread and several pieces of fish, or he got everyone to share the food they were hoarding."

"You don't think getting five thousand strangers to share is a miracle?" Angela said leaning over and lifting the pot bowl.

"I do," I said. "That is the miracle. No one since has been able to get the rich to share their wealth. At least not willingly."

"Zach's right," Samm laughed. "Tony's pot bowl rule makes him like Jesus."

I was going to say that wasn't my point, but that would be disagreeing with Samm in front of everyone, and I liked that she seemed to be fitting in.

"Tony's pot bowl makes him Jesus-like. But his hair, that makes him look like Jesus," Mel said, running her fingers through Tony's shoulder length blond hair.

"And because he's bringing us all together," Angela added. "Jews, Catholics, Episcopalians, atheists. All of us together in harmony getting high and getting along."

"Our own little Woodstock," Mel said.

Turtle came back into the room and unpacked a guitar. He began to play along with the Buffalo Springfield album on the record player. He was so good that Mel handed me the joint she was holding and went to turn off the record player. Turtle gave Mel a cue and she picked up where Stephen Stills had left off, singing about the virtues of kind women and how much our future depended on the kind of women we would each find.

Mel could sing. Flat out sing. She made that song hers and she made it real.

Then this guy Wurm poked his head into the room. "Far out," he shouted. He pulled out the drumsticks that were always in his back pocket and looked around the room. He found a big art book and sat on the floor with the book in front of him and added a beat.

I asked Samm if she wished she had her cello. She said she liked being the audience and that she liked hearing Mel sing.

A guy I'd never seen before sat down next to Amy and apologized for being late. I guess she didn't mind because she gave him a big, long kiss. I listened to the music for a little while longer, but my mouth was dry, and I went with Samm into the kitchen and found some sodas.

As I drank, I stared out the kitchen window at the streetlights and car lights along Queens Boulevard. From six floors up they were mesmerizing. There seemed to be some sort of random order to everything from up above.

"Cool view," Samm said. "Come on." She lifted the pane and went out through the kitchen window. I followed her onto the fire escape.

"An even better view," she said.

"Outstanding," I said.

Samm lit a joint. "You're quite smart."

"I don't know."

"It wasn't a question," she said.

"Okay." I had no idea how to respond. "Thanks?"

"That might be the only thing you don't know," she laughed. "Let's do a shotgun."

Samm put the lit end of the joint between her teeth and pulled my face close hers. I was supposed to put the other end in my mouth and inhale, but all I could think was that her hands felt great on my face and she smelled great. Samm signaled me to hurry which made sense given that the lit part was in her mouth. I put my lips on the end of the joint and cupped my hands onto both our cheeks to create a tunnel and sucked on the joint while she blew the smoke from her end into my mouth. It was amazing and intense. She took the joint out and we exhaled and laughed and then and we did the whole thing again in the opposite direction. We sat and finished the joint the usual way.

Samm leaned forward against the fire escape railing and looked down at the street below.

"Do you wish I had big breasts like those two girls?" Samm said.

"What?"

"Don't stall," she said. "Just answer."

"I like your size breasts," I said. "They're perfect."

"I don't believe you," she said.

"First of all," I said, "I like them because they come with you."

"Good answer," Samm laughed. "And?"

"And what?"

"You said first of all."

"Right. Big breasts are not my thing."

"Aren't they every guy's thing?"

"No. We're all perverts in our own way."

We kissed for a while and then Samm pulled away. "Did you really have to have a piece of your penis cut off?" Samm asked me.

"I see we've started a new topic."

"We have." Samm smiled and leaned her shoulder into mine. We were discussing my penis like it wasn't attached to me.

"They just cut some skin off the top. They don't, you know, cut off a piece of the actual penis."

"Kind of adds new meaning to, give me some skin."

I laughed. "That's funny," I said.

"Did it hurt?"

"Probably, but I was eight days old. It's not an image I like to think about."

"So they don't make it shorter?" Samm said. When I didn't laugh, she did. "Come on, man, I'm kidding. I know what foreskin is. I've just never seen one."

"Foreskin?"

"A hoodless penis," Samm said. "Without a turtleneck." She stood up suddenly, but not that steadily, and balanced herself on my shoulder. "Get up. I want to see yours."

"Here?"

"Yeah," she offered me her hand and helped me up.

A lot of things were going through my mind, but then I was looking at Samm who was looking at my jeans as I undid the zipper. I pulled out my penis, and she leaned in to get a closer look. Then she put her hand on it and felt all around the head.

"Fucking weird," she said. She looked up at me, "no, not your penis. It's just so different. Have you seen the other kind?"

"Sure," I said.

Samm was still holding it. She seemed calm. I was not.

"Where?" she said. "Oh, it likes to be held."

She was right about that. "Locker rooms," I said.

"Right." She looked down again. "It's growing." She started stroking it, and it didn't take long before I came all over the fire escape.

"That was fun," she said.

I was mostly smiling.

Back in the kitchen, we drank glasses of water, and I tried to stop grinning. Music was still being played in the living room. Samm and I went to see. A couple of new guys were jamming along with Turtle and Wurm. Someone else was singing with Mel and they were good together. Better than good. We went over and sat with Jonah and Lu on the couch.

Tony came up behind us and put his arm around me and Jonah. "Let's go to the Stage Diner," he whispered.

"Sure," Lu said.

"You do realize there's a house full of people?" I said.

"I love this guy," Tony said hugging me with both arms. "Always has my back." Then, he went over and whispered in Mel's ear. She stopped singing and the musicians followed suit. Tony put the pot bowl on the floor and stepped up onto the coffee table.

"Party is over people. The cops are on their way here right now," he yelled. "Everyone needs to leave now before they get here and haul your ass to jail. Take what you brought and grab it fast. But leave the weed."

"They'll be frisking you if they stop you outside," Mel added.

"Get the hell out of here people," Tony yelled. "It's been great." He jumped off the table. "Zach, get the stairwell door and send everyone down the stairs. Jonah, block the elevator. It will take all day for everyone to leave by elevator and my baby is hungry."

Lu pulled open Tony's front door and Jonah and Samm and I ran out just ahead of the surging crowd and Samm and I directed kids down the stairwell. After the last of the guests started down the stairwell, Tony locked up the apartment.

"Our carriage awaits," Jonah said, holding the elevator door open for us.

We reached the lobby before the last kids had made it all the way down the six flights of stairs.

"I'm in the mood for pancakes," Tony said, once we were outside. "We should all get pancakes. We should order every type of pancake they have and share. That's what we should do."

"Pancakes it is. I'm fucking starving," Mel said taking the joint from Tony. "How about you, Samm?"

"I could eat."

There was a crowd at the Stage. Typical for a Saturday night. But we got seated fast because they liked to put six in a booth over couples.

Brucie, our favorite late night waiter, came over. He wiped off the table by pushing all the crumbs and leftover food onto the floor. He paused and looked at us for effect. "I do tables, not floors," he said. And as if on cue, a busboy came over and swept the floor around our booth.

"He's funny," Samm said. "You're funny," she told Brucie.

"And your pupils are dilated," he said looking around. "In fact, all your pupils are dilated." Then he pointed to me and said, "How's your birdie, Brucie?" He didn't wait for a response and turned to Mel. "Ok, Brucie, what are you having?" He called everyone Brucie and told us that he was a non-practicing alcoholic.

No one ordered pancakes. After Brucie left we wondered if he was higher than us or not high at all and that we were so high he seemed high. We concluded that it didn't matter.

"There is no such thing as bad French fries," Jonah said when the food arrived.

Later, after our plates had been emptied, Brucie came by with the check. "This one time, my dog ate a box of crayons, and I had Technicolor shit all over my backyard for weeks," he said. "It was groovy."

That was our signal to vacate the booth.

I looked at Samm and Tony and Mel and thought to myself that life was indeed groovy.

• • •

The Mets went on to sweep the Braves and just like that they were heading to the World Series where they would play the powerful Baltimore Orioles. They lost their first game with Seaver on the mound, but Jonah and I did not lose faith. Not completely. Especially when they evened the series the next day. And on Tuesday they took the lead, two games to one. And then Seaver took the mound for the second time on Wednesday, and he pitched ten innings and with the help of Ron Swoboda's amazing catch, the Mets were suddenly one win away from a world championship.

On Thursday, Jonah and I walked to school without mentioning the Mets. You don't mess with a streak. You don't tempt the baseball gods, and we didn't want to do anything to jinx the Mets. It was clear to us, that any false move on our part would have a direct influence on the outcome. Why risk it?

By the time I got to math class later that day, the Mets were losing 3-0 in the third inning. No one said it would be easy. Mr. Steel placed his radio on his desk and told us to listen. There were some kids in the class who were not baseball fans, who did not follow sports, who did not understand. Mr. Steel made it simple for them. He said baseball was math and imagination and poetry all wrapped inside 108 stitches. And, he added, he was the teacher, so deal with it. That was when I pulled out my hat from my bag and asked Lisa to put it on.

She looked at Mr. Steel.

"The question is, why did you wait so long?' he said.

"Baseball fans are way too superstitious," Lisa said.

"Are there levels of superstition?" Mr. Steel said.

After she put the hat on, Koosman found his rhythm on the mound and little Al Weiss who had hit just two home runs all year turned physics into poetry and tied the game with a blast over the left field fence. We listened till the bell rang signaling the end of the school day. Mr. Steel told us we could stay and listen to the game. I was glad when Lisa said she wanted to stay.

"What happened?" Jonah said, running into Mr. Steel's room. He pulled a chair next to me as Cleon Jones and Ron Swoboda and Gerry Grote did their thing and the Mets took the lead.

Jonah and I shouted.

"It's a little silly, right?" Lisa asked Jonah. "I mean they're math guys. They trust numbers. I'm sitting here in a high school classroom, and they think that if I keep this hat on…" Lisa raised her hand toward the hat.

"Do not touch that hat," all of us yelled.

She lowered her hand.

"And we absolutely should not be talking about this during the game," Jonah said. "Never mess with a streak. How do you not already know that?"

"Okay," she said. "But you're all crazy. Certifiably."

"I'm okay with that diagnosis as long as you keep the hat on your head," I said.

Koosman kept getting outs, and all of sudden there was just that last one left to get. But you couldn't think of it that way. Ever. Not even for a second. A lot can happen before the last out. You play the whole game. You play all 27 outs. You don't tempt fate. You don't press your luck. Outs don't have clocks. You wait for the Fat Lady to sing before you even think about uncorking champagne. Before you even look at the champagne.

And while I was thinking, Davey Johnson lifted a fly ball to left. The announcer did not say that Cleon Jones had to fade back. He said that

Jones was standing in left field waiting. And we stood, too, waiting for gravity to do its thing and bring that baseball to rest in his glove. That was that. Game over. Twenty-seven outs.

And then there was nothing. The world went silent. Until Jonah jumped on me, hugging me and screaming and smiling and Mr. Steel came over and shook all our hands.

Lisa turned to me and smiled. She hugged me and asked, "Now?"

"Yes, now," I said.

Lisa removed my hat and threw it up in the air.

Jonah yelled and slapped my back again and again and neither of us seemed to know what to say to each other and neither of us could stop smiling.

Lisa caught my hat and offered it back to me.

"You keep it," I said. "It's a good luck charm."

"I'll keep it to remind me that we shared this moment." Then Lisa hugged me again. "Can't wait to see my dad," she whispered. She kind of sounded like she was crying.

Mr. Steel offered us a ride home. Lisa left to meet some friends and Jonah and I followed Mr. Steel to his van.

The inside of Mr. Steel's van just had a middle and rear bench and Jonah and I sat together in the middle. I think I was disappointed, though I'm not sure what I was expecting. It would have been creepy if there was a bed in it instead of just a lot of seats. We spent the ride talking about the Mets' season, remembering our favorite moments. We celebrated every moment of the way home. Every. Single. Moment. Because all was right with the world. The Mets were world champions. And somehow, that reflected on me and Jonah. I just wasn't sure how.

Back in my room on the radio, Paul Jacobs didn't even want to play music, he just wanted to talk Mets. And he didn't mention the war once that day.

• • •

The war in the jungle continued to drag on and felt unwinnable. The same could be said for the war at home. The Chicago-Seven drama was underway, and they were putting the war on trial. But the thing that totally bothered me was that the case pitted radical Abbie Hoffman against establishment Judge Julius Hoffman. It was a Jewish judge presiding over a Jewish defendant who was being represented by a Jewish lawyer, William Kunstler. Hoffman, Rubin, and Weiner made the defendants sound like a law firm or a Jewish conspiracy. It looked like every defendant was Jewish. Clearly, there was no way this ended well for Jews. Every way you looked at it, we lose.

And the totals in my notebook kept rising steadily.

The Mets' celebrations had all but faded as the war intruded back into everything. It was swift and it was harsh. News broke about the investigation into the potential court-martial of Lieutenant William Calley Jr. for having led a massacre of pretty much every person in the village of My Lai in Quang Ngai Province. The details were gruesome and graphic. Calley and his men had endured a brutal battle with the Viet Cong and had suffered horrific losses. Instead of being brought back to base, they remained in the jungle, and were sent into My Lai to search for VC. When they didn't find any, they carried out a series of savage acts against the villagers. They were in search of revenge, and I was in search of every detail I could find about the boys of 1st Platoon, Company C, 1st Battalion, 20th Infantry Regiment, 11th Infantry Brigade, 23rd Infantry Division – Calley's platoon.

A few things became clear to me right away.

First. There was no way this was a unique, one-time incident. This was just the one that got noticed. The one that got someone's attention.

Second. If we were going to hold those men of Calley's platoon responsible for their actions in the jungle, well, and I kept coming back to this question, shouldn't we also hold accountable the politicians who voted for the war, the generals who gave the orders, and the voters who elected the politicians who voted to fund the war. Should we hold accountable everyone who stood by and did nothing? And I knew, that meant I was at fault, I was guilty, too.

And third. And this was the harshest to accept. The more I read about what happened that quiet afternoon, the more I heard about the details that leaked from the investigation, the more I could not be sure that if I had been on patrol with those men, the more sure I was that I would not have been able to abstain; I was increasingly certain that I would have joined them in their rage. I was, in fact, becoming increasingly convinced that I would have snapped like those young boys of C Company. And it scared me.

And then I thought about David and Frankie and Sal and I wondered what they had participated in. I wondered what they had seen. The memories that David carried home with him had stopped him from sleeping. Were they more traumatic than what Frankie and Sal had been through? Were they as disturbing as what Calley's platoon had seen…and done??

And then I understood what Samm did not want to know.

I wondered what had happened to these men of C Company that let them do this? What scared me was that I was sure it could happen to me.

I started thinking about what kind of training was needed to prepare one to fight in a war. To learn to kill. Was that how the Nazis turned Germans into cold-blooded murder machines?

Is this what turned German school principals, teachers, prison guards, police, priests, and even parents, into sadists.

But, mostly, I wondered why anyone was surprised that this had happened. Why was anyone surprised at all?

• • •

The weather was starting to change when I met Samm in Washington Square. She thought it might be her last outside gig for the season. It was getting too cold for her hands to play, for her cello to be outside, and even for people to linger and dawdle in the park.

After she played, we went to Dante, but it was so packed that we found another coffee shop along McDougal and had cheese with apples as we sipped Americanos. Afterwards, I carried Samm's cello and followed as she led me through the Village. We stopped at The Kettle of Fish, a one time regular hang out for the Beats. Samm was surprised I'd never read *On The Road.* The bouncer wouldn't let us into the bar even when Samm told him that I was visiting from Lowell, Massachusetts, that I was related to Jack Kerouac, and that she just wanted me to get a chance to see the place, not to get a drink. He laughed and told her that she must be the one related to Kerouac because that was quite a story. Then he stepped aside and told us we had three minutes.

After, Samm led me across the street into Sheridan Square and we sat on a bench and made out. Then she asked me if I wanted to borrow her copy of *On The Road.*

"I would," I said.

"Let's go get it."

"Now?" I asked. "Tonight?"

"Yes." Samm stood. "I have one in my room. And my parents aren't home."

"Okay," I jumped up. "Yes. Let's go."

"Wait for me," Samm laughed.

The hallway to her room was filled with pictures of Samm at different ages and she had a cello in most of them. She had a bunch of pictures of her brother in her room and a stack of letters from David on her desk. She stopped talking to me about David after he told her that he wanted to return to Vietnam. She was worried, but at the same time, she was trying to make peace with the idea that he might need to return.

"Do you ever worry that you might stop liking the cello?"

"No." She removed her copy of *On The Road* from her bookshelf.

"Because you can't imagine not loving it?"

"Because if I do," Samm said, "it will mean I found something I love even more."

"And you won't regret or resent all that time you spent practicing?"

"Are we talking about math?

"Maybe," I said.

"You think there's a finite number of things you can love?"

"Love? No. But to be an expert? Yes," I said.

"It's about passion. It's about paying attention to something. The process changes you. So, no. No regrets." Samm dropped the needle onto Santana. "No regrets."

"Okay." I sat next to her.

Samm looked at me for a while and then said, "What were we just talking about?"

"Not having regrets."

"Exactly."

"I feel like you have a point."

"I do."

"And I'm missing it."

"You are," Samm said, and then didn't say anything.

"I'm sitting next to you on your bed in an empty house and you just told me to not have regrets."

"And you're still talking and not kissing me?"

"I should kiss you?"

"You should stop talking."

I kissed Samm and we fell back onto her bed which was followed by clumsy clothing removal, awkward body positioning, and frantic exploration of skin. My hands found endless bumps and crevices and curves that moved toward me, away from me. Samm's hands explored my body, touching places that rarely got touched.

"So we're going to have sex?" I said. "Like now?"

"See, you are smart," Samm laughed. "Have you done it before?"

"No."

"Smart and honest," she said.

"You?"

"No."

"Cool," I said. I should have been nervous, but Samm was so comfortable she made me feel almost comfortable.

"I don't have a condom," I said, pulling my lips away from hers.

"I'm on the pill," Samm said, pulling my head back toward her.

"But you're Catholic," I said.

"I'm not."

"But those crosses."

"Episcopalian," Samm said. "But only on my parents' side."

And then I was inside her. And all the smells and sounds and tastes and sights and touches from each of my senses battled for attention. And then suddenly the sensory overload disappeared and feeling and being felt became one. And I stopped thinking. Completely stopped. There was not a thought happening, not even in the most remote chamber of my brain. Not even the thought that there was not a thought. And it was good. It was outstanding good. It was beyond words good. It was beyond meaning good.

We just were.

And then it was over.

We lay on the bed looking up at the ceiling. "Sorry," I said.

"For what?"

"You know. That was sort of quick. Quick, but spectacular. I mean, look at you."

Samm laughed.

"You know, you don't get to do things for the first time a second time so I hope you're not disappointed."

"That's crap," Samm said.

"Which part?"

"The first time doing anything almost always sucks. It's fucking cool that it happened, that you tried something, but you're never, or almost never good at something the first time. Let's do it again."

"Yes, please."

The second time we moved around and changed positions and took a bit longer. It was a more wonderful thing than the first time.

"You're the smart one," I said. "Much better than the first time. How does everyone not just do this all the time," I said. If this isn't heaven, I thought, then I don't need to go.

Samm laughed.

"Seriously," I said. "And another thing, I never really fully truly understood what people meant by 'Make Love Not War' before. What an easy choice."

"Okay, Zach, what did I tell you about talking too much?"

"Not to?"

"Right."

"Or I'll regret it," I added.

I thought I had said something wrong, but she told me that she wasn't done and then she showed me how to help her finish.

"You are cute," Samm said, kissing me on the cheek. "I'm glad it was you."

"Me, too," I said. "I mean that it was you. I'm really glad it was me, too."

I wanted to stay in Samm's room, in her bed, in her arms, in her, forever and ever and ever and ever and ever. Which was when she looked at her clock and casually mentioned that if I stayed around much longer I would get to meet her parents. She laughed as I practically fell out of bed to gather my clothes. I began to dress with even more speed and determination than I had undressed. Samm was still laughing when

I looked up. I liked seeing her sitting on her bed. Naked.

"I could get used to this," I said.

"Me, too."

"And I regret nothing," I told Samm when I left.

On the subway, I cracked open *On The Road* and read and read. Yes.

Samm was right. Yes.

I read on and on. The words beat against the endless current of the subway, wheels rolling against the tracks.

Yes, madness.

Yes, Kerouac.

Yes, Sal Paradise.

"Sex IS holy," I said out loud.

Yes, Dean Moriarty.

Yes. Yes. Yes. Yes, Samm.

A thousand yeses.

RAMBLE ON

I heard Jonah downstairs playing chess with my father. It was not unusual for him to come early and talk with my dad, and often they had a game of chess. My father taught Jonah to play just like he had taught me. At times, we would set up two boards and each played a game against my father at the same time.

Jonah and I were planning to watch the Jets game at my house after we got high. They had won the Super Bowl the year before which was as unlikely and amazing as the Mets' World Series win. But this season, they sucked again. We hoped that wouldn't happen to the Mets. Winning was more fun than sucking. My house was where we watched TV together when we watched TV together because we never watched TV together at Jonah's house.

I slipped on a t-shirt and jeans, grabbed my black canvas high-tops, and headed downstairs.

"Zach, tell your Dad to let me win," Jonah said.

"You're not a baby anymore," my father responded.

"I am," Jonah said.

"He is," I added, sitting next to Jonah. I tried to help him.

"I've taught you how to win. Letting you win teaches you nothing."

"But I like winning."

"When you win, you will see it many moves before the game ends. And that will be truly fun."

"You think I'll get good enough to beat you?" Jonah asked.

"Me?" my father said. "No. Other people."

"Like Zach?"

"Sure. Why not? He stopped playing."

"I didn't stop," I said, tying my sneakers. "I just haven't had time."

Chess was something we did together, me and my dad. The game was a rare father-son-polio-free zone. For a while, I tried to get my dad to come down to the park and play with the neighborhood men, most of them immigrants, who had unofficially laid claim to a corner of the park on weekends. My father had no interest. I would have liked to see him leaning over as he contemplated the whole board and planned his next several moves. And then, for a few moments, I would not be that kid who pushes his father in a wheelchair, but a son watching his father play chess. Also, he was good and he deserved to play the game with equals who shared his love for the game. But he preferred to play against me, so I stopped asking.

When I turned seven and again at eight, I blew out birthday candles and wished that my father's polio would be cured. In between candle blowing, I tried pulling on wishbones and tossing pennies into fountains. On the high holidays, I tried praying, but synagogue never resonated with me. I usually just fell asleep. It's not like we were particularly observant. If you pressed me, I would say my parents were atheists. More agnostic. Though they would not likely admit it. Anyway, curing his polio didn't seem like a lot to ask for from that person who created it. All I wanted was to walk into Shea Stadium, my father's arm around my shoulder as he guided us to our seats, where we would share peanuts and watch the Mets.

That Yom Kippur, I forgave god and added the opportunity for god to atone. Nothing happened. Up on my roof, I looked toward the sky and offered to negotiate. Maybe a cure was too much? Was having a catch or taking a stroll down our block too much? What precisely was not too much, I wondered? What would be acceptable to both god and my father? Was it letting him walk for a year? A month? A week? A day? What about a single hour? How many steps would be worth it before my father wished he had never remembered what it felt like to walk again? I began to wonder if he would have wanted the opportunity to walk for a day if he knew that each step brought him closer to returning to the confinement of his wheelchair.

Clearly, I lacked the clout to get god's attention, so I gave up seeking god's help. And then I gave up seeking god. I mean, if there was a god with the ability to make my father walk again, then why would that god let him get polio in the first place. Why allow for any disease? Or assholes? Or the Holocaust? Or the disparity between the Yankees and Mets?

At best, creation had been botched. A hack job. A random experiment. Just a few moments after god announced that it was all good, the main characters, the only characters of Genesis, told the first lie and committed the first murder. Things were such a mess that god quickly took a mulligan, a do-over. A flood was sent to cleanse his new toy and start fresh. When that didn't pan out, god found Abraham and told him that he had won some lottery and from that moment forward it would be on him and his descendants to fix crap. I think Abraham was god's exit strategy. But that's not how god sold it to Abraham. It was like Abraham was getting a promotion with a title bump. But it was a ruse. There wasn't any pay raise or added perks. It was just do what god said, or else you'd better run.

Call it incompetence or boredom, but god couldn't even get the lineage right and Abraham was ordered to banish his first son, Ishmael, in favor of his second son, Isaac, thereby starting an endless senseless bloody sibling rivalry. Who does that?

The stories did have some seriously twisted humor. Like when Abraham was summoned to fetch Isaac and climb the mountain to offer a sacrifice to god. They reached the top and Isaac looked around, took inventory of the ritual altar, saw the slaughter knife in his father's hand, and innocently muttered the scariest words in the bible: *But where's the lamb?*

That same god let me waste perfectly good birthday wishes trying to undo something that should never have been done. I couldn't understand how anyone believed in any god. Seemed to me that belief in one god was the same as belief in any of the others. I no longer had faith in any deity, wishbones, reincarnation, the tooth fairy, Zeus, angels, Santa Claus, or even the alignment of the planets. No one was playing dice with the universe, so I gave up on birthday wishes, too.

I never asked my father for his opinion on this subject. I didn't want to know how he felt about not walking, how he felt about being stuck in a chair for the rest of his life. I didn't want to ask if he remembered what it felt like to walk or run.

I should have realized that my father was angry, but not bitter. Given the chance, clearly he would have taken the opportunity to walk for a day, even while being constantly aware that each passing second brought him closer to returning to his chair because every step would also have been full of possibility. Because he also knew that no one ever knows with certainty how long they'll be walking.

"It's over," Jonah said, laying down his king.

While I had not been able to help Jonah defeat my father, it took longer for him to lose with me by his side.

"It was over nine moves ago," I said.

"When you traded your knight for my bishop. You exposed your rook and left a hole in your defense," my father said.

"But bishops are more valuable than knights," Jonah said.

"On paper, yes. But at that moment, keeping your knight was more valuable to you than taking my bishop. Every piece has a significance on its own, but also in context. Each piece can make a difference," my father said. "You can't always predict what will end up mattering until you play the game."

"We've stopped talking about chess," I said.

"Every move you make, every choice you make, changes everything that follows."

I told my father that we would play soon. He said he was looking forward to it. Then I followed Jonah out of my house toward the Little League fields. We turned onto Short Street, a dead end with three houses on either side, and then onto the path that led to Hernia Hill. At the bottom, we crossed the two sets of the no longer in use railroad tracks and walked onto the last of the four baseball fields.

In sixth grade, our last year in Little League, Jonah and I were on the same team. He was the best player in the league. I was fast, even faster than Jonah, but that was it. I was a shaky fielder and an inconsistent hitter. I blamed it on my lousy eyesight. Nobody cared for any excuses. Either you could play or you couldn't. I played right field when I got to play. Right field was where they played you if you couldn't play. And if you played there long enough you never would be able to. Coach probably wouldn't have played me at all except the rules said everyone had to play. Because of Jonah, we won the league championship. Winning was fun.

The Little League didn't mow the grass in the summer since there weren't any scheduled games, and when we were younger, those fields became whatever Jonah and I could imagine. If we had ice cream, we brought it to the field and sat in the shade of the dugout eating slowly. The slower the better. All summer we wanted to slow things down, we wanted to keep our ice cream from melting, the sun from setting, summer from ending. We used the dugout as a sundial; time could be told with reasonable accuracy by following the length of the shadow covering third base. When the shadow reached shortstop it was time to leave our fields and head home for dinner; back to our houses where we were children and where our day was over.

Several years back, a donation from the Mets had saved the fields from being turned into apartments. It was now a permanent baseball park. And while we no longer played ball on those fields, it remained a sanctuary for Jonah and me. As we sat in the dugout and smoked a joint that day, the fields seemed small and the games were fading memories of a time long gone when we were so much younger.

"We both have girlfriends," Jonah said as we climbed back up Hernia Hill.

We started laughing so hard that we had to rest half way up.

"Why is that funny?" I asked, laughing.

"I don't know. But it is."

When we stopped laughing, we decided we were starving. Not in that I haven't eaten in days starving, but that insatiable, singularly focused in the moment, starving. We turned away from our houses in the direction of the supermarket. Once inside, while staring at some Yoohoos, we remembered that neither of us had any money.

"I'll race you to your house," Jonah said, as he took off running down the aisle and out the store.

I took off after him.

"I hope your mother restocked the vanilla syrup," he called back to me.

"I'm craving cereal," I said, catching up and passing him.

• • •

Back in my kitchen, I grabbed a bowl and cereal. Jonah poked around inside the snack cabinet.

My mom came in.

"Mrs. H.," Jonah said to my mother, "you're out of vanilla syrup." He was the only one who called her that.

"Add it to the list," she said.

"How am I supposed to make my vanilla egg cream?" he laughed.

"You can't," my mom laughed. "You'll have to make chocolate."

"But I like vanilla more."

"Add it to the list," she repeated. My mom loved it when Jonah said stuff like that to her. If I said it, she'd send me to the store with the list.

Jonah made a chocolate egg cream, grabbed some newspaper, and sat next to me. I was staring at an ad suggesting membership in the American Automobile Association. Triple A. Like minor league baseball. The ad showed a car driving along a tree-lined country road at peak fall foliage and it promised to help drivers escape the city and find freedom on the open road. They offered to help plan my fall getaway and to provide maps and guidebooks.

"What's an open road," I asked Jonah. "Is that like toll-free?"

"The Knicks are off to a great start," Jonah said. "You got to love Nate Bowman. Hits a ten foot jumper. Then he misses a two-foot hook shot by three feet."

I looked up at Jonah. "What?" I had no idea how long I'd been staring at the paper and I couldn't remember what we were talking about. I was focused on the Triple A ad. It was a sign. It seemed so obvious. This was my part. I needed to find the open road. I needed to be ready to help my family escape when the US decided it was their time to round up its Jews. That was what my grandfather was trying to tell me. That was why he kept his passport by the door for me to see. It had been a year since my Bar Mitzvah and I had been putting up bagels. I had not come up with a single idea as to what my part, my role, was, and now, it was right in front of me. I needed to know every road and path out of the neighborhood. I needed to find an escape route for my family. I needed to be prepared and ready.

"I'm going to take up running," I said. "I'm going to try out for the track team in the spring so I'm going to start running now to get in shape and be ready."

"Cause you can't hit a curveball," Jonah said.

"Right."

"Or a fastball."

"Sure."

"But you are pretty fast."

"And it would be fun to play a sport in high school. To be on a team."

"Here's the thing," Jonah said. "Running is not a sport. You don't play running."

"Are you saying runners aren't athletes?"

"Of course they're athletes. But running is not a sport. There's no defense. You need defense."

"Ping pong?"

"Sure. It's like shrunken tennis," Jonah said. "But sure."

"Chess?"

"Game. Not a sport. Cards. Checkers. Yahtzee. Games. Unless you can hit the other runners while you go around the track, it's not a sport."

I wanted to make sure I didn't let Jonah know I was thinking about escape routes out of America. "Yahtzee is a funny word," I said.

"Game 7 of the World Series," Jonah said. "Koufax is up against the Twins."

"I know the game."

"Couple innings in and everyone knew he had no curveball. He even stopped throwing it."

"Again. I know the game."

"All he had was one pitch. His fastball. And every Twin hitter knew it was coming on every pitch and he still beat them."

"That was a great game," I said. I had to know what was coming and I had to be able to react.

"You can't do that with running. If you are off your game or are sick you will lose."

"Well, I'm still going out for the track team."

"You should," Jonah said.

"And you'll go running with me to get me ready."

"Sure. But when you're on the track team and I'm on the baseball team I will be sure to remind you every day that while I'll be playing a game, you'll just be getting exercise."

• • •

By Halloween, I had run through every alley, down every street, along every railroad track, through every backyard. I looked for caves and tunnels to hide in. I came up empty. Running revealed nothing except that I liked running. Like my dad. It agreed with me. And I was good at it. That much was clear.

It was also clear that I had failed to find an escape route out of the neighborhood. The one task I set out to accomplish led me to discover what I already knew. The world was impossible to navigate in a wheelchair.

I decided to take a different approach to the problem. I needed to be able to spot the signs ahead of everyone else. It was like a chess game in which I didn't know what moves to look for or prepare for. Almost every Jew in Europe, almost every person in the world, had missed the signs when Hitler and his friends slipped into elected offices in Germany. How was I supposed to be better at reading the national tea leaves than everyone else?

• • •

On Wednesday, I called Ali from Jonah's house. I was getting used to talking to her. She seemed to be interested in what I was up to, and I liked telling her things that were on my mind even when I didn't know what I thought. I liked knowing she was safe.

That Wednesday, she told me about The Moratorium March to end the war in Vietnam that was coming up in DC. Ali was part of a group at Columbia that was helping organize buses to get people to the protest. People were going to show up from all over, she said, and she wanted me to come along with her. She thought it was important that I go, that I show up and be counted. She offered to get me and Jonah bus tickets.

Samm was all in when I called her about DC. The next day in the cafeteria Jonah said the Moratorium would be our Woodstock and that we all must go together.

"Are you saying I should go with you?" Lu said to Jonah.

"Yes."

"You're asking me on an actual date?"

"It's a demonstration," Jonah said, "so not a date."

"But you're asking me to go with you?"

"I was saying we should go together."

"And we'll sit on the bus together?"

"Definitely."

"And we'll hang out in DC?" Lu said.

"Yes."

"Together?"

"That's right," Jonah said.

"But it is not a date?" Lu laughed.

"Exactly."

"I don't understand, but I love it," she said.

"How great is she," Jonah said, hugging Lu and looking at me.

Mel couldn't go because of her parents' anniversary, and Tony had a baptism or confirmation. Something at church.

When I mentioned going to DC to my parents, they were okay with the idea. When I told them I would be going with Ali my mother said that was nice, and my father looked sad. I thought they might change their mind, but my Dad gave me money to pay for my ticket and for

Ali's. He said to make sure she was okay, and to tell her that they missed her and she should come visit.

• • •

Samm was coming to hang out at the schoolyard with all of us and Jonah came with me to meet her at the subway. We shuffled down Hernia Hill, then Jonah took off running, and we raced each other alongside the railroad tracks to the 63rd Drive overpass where we jumped onto the sidewalk, laughing as we turned right and headed towards Anthony's Pizza like we had thousands of times before. Except on that October afternoon, I saw the same sign again. First there was that ad in the paper. And now, right across the street from the overpass was a giant Triple A sign was being fastened to the facade of a new branch of the American Automobile Association. Another sign in the window announced a Grand Opening for the following Saturday.

Finally, a sign so large and obvious that even I couldn't miss it. I needed to join the Triple A club and collect every bit of information they possessed about the roads and routes, about the bridges and tunnels, about every interstate and backroad of this great land from the New York Islands to California. I needed to know everything they knew. They would be my guides, my mentors. They would show me the way out. The path to safety. But I would never tell them that was what they were doing.

"What," Jonah said.

"Just catching my breath," I said.

"I thought you were in shape," he said.

And then I darted ahead of him to Anthony's where we had pizza. That day it tasted better than usual.

• • •

The following Saturday I took a number at the new Triple A office and waited for my turn to stand in front of a lady who started asking me a lot of questions. I didn't want questions, I wanted answers. I wanted to give her money, and have her give me maps. But they needed an address to mail me my membership card and any maps they didn't stock.

"It's a post office. box," I told her, "and I can't remember it."

"You don't have a street address?" She wasn't buying.

"It's an anniversary present for my parents," I said. "They never had a honeymoon because, you know, they didn't have the money, and now my sister and I are planning a surprise trip for them to Niagara Falls. We want it to be a surprise, so she got us a post office box. She's at college."

Her stone gaze melted. She suggested that I hurry home and get the box number and come back. She promised to gather all the guidebooks and maps for a trip to Niagara Falls and have them at her desk when I returned. I mentioned that my parents might want to see the Falls from the Canadian side as well. She agreed that they should.

I was pretty happy with myself as I headed for the Post Office to rent a box. I wasn't sure what made me think Canada would take in Jews, but I had to believe they would. After all, they gave refuge to draftees who didn't want to be sent to Vietnam. And Canada was close. Which kind of made Canada our best, if not only, option.

I returned to find a stack of books and maps waiting for me. The woman finished processing my membership and sent me on my way with the promise that my permanent AAA card and a steady stream of maps and guidebooks would arrive at my private collection box.

For the next nine nights, I listened to Jenny on the radio while I read, studied, familiarized, and memorized the meaning of road signs, the names of towns and road crossings, and landmarks that appeared between Queens and the Canadian border.

And I memorized the words to *O Canada.*

BREAK ON THROUGH

I was getting ready to head to the city and catch the bus going to DC for the Moratorium. The caravan was leaving at midnight in front of the big post office on 8th Avenue, and the plan was for me, Jonah, and Lu to meet up with Samm and Ali by the 31st Street end of the pillars at the top of the steps.

I stood in front of my bathroom sink, staring into the mirror, looking for something to shave. That was when I heard Paul Jacobs announce that he was doing his last show. Just like that. Not last for the week. Not last before he left for vacation. Just last. No warning, no buildup, no promos, no farewell shows. No speech. No words of advice or parting sentiments. He was moving on. Paul didn't say why he was leaving or where he was going. I wanted to tell him that I was not okay with his decision. I was not okay with this sudden change at the last moment. And even though I was listening, I was not okay that I might not have been listening, and would not have known what happened to him.

Paul was talking in a calm voice, pulling me into the armchair beside him. He had always been able to make me feel like the city was a small town and we were all neighbors. More importantly, he asked the right questions, had a few answers, and I had started to count on him. I wanted to ask him whom I should turn to in his absence,

I turned up the radio, and though I was only inches away, I strained to catch each word. Desperately, I tried to slow down sound. I tried to make my brain listen in slow motion and record every moment. I tried to break words into syllables, syllables into letters. For a moment, I was sure that I no longer understood English.

I listened to Paul Jacobs talk about the demonstration we were going to, but it didn't sound like he was going to be there. And then he said he was going to sing a song as his farewell. Footsteps echoed inside the radio. A chair scratched across the floor, and then the sound of piano keys struck. Paul began to sing about birds and wires and drunks and about trying to be free. The song ended, and he thanked everyone for listening, and was off.

It all happened so fast. One of those rare moments, those times that you could actually define as the instant before and the instant after. It was not some subtle slide toward something. Nor was it a series of declarations or decisions leading to doing. Just the moment before I knew Paul was going off the air. Followed immediately by the instant I knew he stopped being available to me.

I pulled the plug which disconnected the radio so that it no longer turned on with the light. When I got dressed, I picked out only black clothing. Black t-shirt, black jeans, black socks, and my black canvas high-tops. I suddenly had one less adult I could rely on. I grabbed my jacket and was off to get Jonah.

• • •

A crowd had already formed on the west side of 8th Avenue in front of the post office by the time Lu and Jonah and I arrived. There were four buses lined up along 8th Avenue and they all said Washington, DC above their windshield.

I saw Samm and Ali hanging out together up on the steps. Ali waved to us as we approached. Samm skipped down a few steps and gave me a kiss and a hug. Then she reached into her bag and removed a pretzel.

"I got this across the street," Samm said. "It looked promising."

"Oh no," Jonah said, "she's joined the quest."

"Don't encourage him," Ali said.

"What's that all about?" Lu asked.

"You don't want to know," Jonah said.

Ali hugged me and whispered in my ear. "She's great, and she totally likes you…for some reason."

On the bus, Jonah and Lu took seats near the front, but Samm wanted to keep looking, so I followed her down the aisle. She stopped suddenly, and told me to slide into a window seat. The bus went dark and the driver made his way up 8th Avenue toward the Lincoln Tunnel. Traffic was light, and we quickly emerged from the Hudson River and turned south onto the New Jersey Turnpike. We settled in for the ride.

That guy Turtle from my birthday party at Tony's was on the bus. He pulled out his guitar and started playing. A harmonica joined in, and Turtle started singing about having sunshine and warmth on cold and cloudy days. And I was so happy to be sitting there with my girl. Around the bus, others sang along. I was not tempted to join in.

"Paul Jacobs signed off from his show," I told Samm. "He sang a song on air and then he signed off. No explanation."

"You sound angry," she said.

"He just left."

"He betrayed you?" she asked me, clearly unimpressed by my devastation.

"Not just me."

"You think he owes you something?" Samm said.

"No."

"And now you're mad at him."

"He shouldn't have let me follow him if he was going to just leave," I said. "What happened to loyalty? To commitment?"

"What song?"

"What?"

"You said he sang a song."

"'Bird On A Wire.'"

"And you don't think there was a message there?"

"Of course there is," I said. "Like what?"

"I don't know. Maybe trying to be free in his own way. Why are you mad at me?" Samm replied.

I was angry and maybe I was thinking she didn't understand. I took a breath. "I'm not angry at you."

"You better not be," she said. "Why that song?"

"I don't know, but there's like maybe only ten songs as good as 'Bird On A Wire.' It has some of the best lines ever written. Leonard Cohen is almost as good as Dylan."

"But you don't think it was a message about leaving the show? About Jacob's trying to be free?"

"Sure, I get that."

"But it's still about you?"

"I don't know how to answer that."

"Which ten?" Samm said.

"Which ten what?"

"What are the other songs?"

"Oh," I said. "*My Back Pages. Desolation Row…*"

"You're just going to name ten Dylan songs?"

"Possibly."

"There's that second part of the song. After trying to be free. The 'if' part. Cohen says if he was unkind, he hopes you can just let it go. If he's been untrue, it was not to his audience. Not to you. You don't get that?"

"I do. But he still left," I said.

"It's impossible to NOT be unkind to those we love. It's only the people we love that care enough to be hurt. If you didn't like his show, then you wouldn't give a crap that he left, and then you wouldn't feel like he wronged you."

"Sure, but then there's the part where he promises to make it right," I said. "It's like Kol Nidre meets Don Quixote."

"He doesn't have to make it right. But maybe he already did. Maybe he already got you to ask for more. Maybe you need to ask for less. Maybe you have to ask for more from someone else. Or from yourself. But not from Jacobs."

"You're more."

"More?"

"More smart, more beautiful, more everything, than I thought I would ever meet," I said.

"There are no grownups," Samm said, not letting me change the subject so easily.

"Talk about a non-sequitur."

"People get older, but everyone is winging it. Especially adults. There isn't anyone to follow. Nobody is leading." Samm said. "Everyone lives with uncertainty."

"I can live with doubt and uncertainty. I prefer it over having what might be the wrong answers. Paul seemed to have answers."

"Not too likely," Samm said. "There are very few answers."

"How do you know?"

"Just look at the mess we're in." Samm kissed me. "Enough talking," she said as the bus crossed the bridge and entered Delaware. "Get up. We're changing seats."

"Why?"

"I want the window."

I followed Samm into the aisle. She removed her jacket, slid across the seat, and faced the window. She laid her jacket across her lap. I sat and Samm took my hand and moved it under her coat and whispered, "I just undid my jeans, so you can do that thing you do so well with your fingers."

"Really?"

"Really."

"And you think I'm good at it?" I smiled as I slid my hand inside her panties.

"Yes."

"Outstanding."

"Do a good job," Samm whispered, "and then you'll get a turn."

As the bus crossed the bridge into Wilmington, I changed seats with Samm. She didn't have to work too hard, and my turn was over before we left Delaware.

"Best bus trip ever," I said, kissing Samm. "And I proclaim that sex is one of the answers."

"To what?" Samm laughed.

"To everything."

• • •

We landed in DC at sunrise. The bus dropped us off behind Union Station. As we de-boarded, we were reminded, warned, that the bus would leave at 5 p.m. sharp, with or without us. Once off the bus, we became part of a swelling crowd making its way along New York Avenue. Along the route folks filed out of Metro stations, side streets, apartments, and parked cars to join in. We were regaled by scripted chants, continuously repeated.

Are you listening, Nixon?

Are you listening, Agnew?

We were told that we were on a march against death.

When the crowd neared the Ellipse, the marchers dispersed and our little group did the same. Ali said she had to find folks from Johns Hopkins who were planning something with her Columbia University committee. Lu wanted to take Jonah to get some breakfast at a diner she had been to with her family. We picked a time and place to meet up later in the day and went our own ways.

I told Samm that I hoped to see the Hamilton statue in front of the Treasury, so we continued to make our way over to 15th Street.

"You're not troubled that the founding fathers owned slaves?" Samm asked.

"I am. But Hamilton didn't own slaves. Still, while many of them did, that small group gathered in Virginia changed the world, and I find them intriguing."

"Is it like how the Nazis gave us the VW bug?"

"I get hypocrisy," I said. "And it's not that I don't care about the owning of slaves thing. I mean it totally contradicts everything else they did. But they left behind a constitution that was able to fix itself, that was able to transcend the time they created it in."

"Which is why it's hard to justify, hard to understand the owning slaves thing."

"What if we dismissed every good idea because the person who created it was flawed, then we would reject every single idea."

"They should have known better," Samm said. "Many people back then knew better."

"You're not wrong. But I don't think we'll ever find a group like that again. And we need them," I said. "We need a better version of them." I need them, I said to myself.

I read the inscription below Hamilton's name out loud. "He was a champion of National Integrity."

Samm wanted to catch Arlo Guthrie who was supposed to be singing early in the program. We made our way over to the Mall where we found an empty patch of grass in the sun, near a sign that suggested dropping acid instead of dropping bombs. Someone was talking, but we weren't listening. Whoever he was didn't matter. He was just droning on and on like white noise.

"These speakers are standing in Lincoln's shadow and they have learned nothing from him," Samm said. "two hundred and seventy two words. That was all Lincoln needed for the Gettysburg Address. And his second inaugural, the one where he talks about malice toward none," Samm was getting angry, "that was just seven hundred and one words. More was definitely less. Now, that is some real math."

"So, they teach you more than just music at that school of yours."

Before she could reply, the speaker introduced Pete Seeger and Arlo Guthrie who came out in front of a roar to perform John Lennon's "Give Peace A Chance." The crowd joined in, and Samm stood up to get a better view.

I stood up with her and noticed a lot of people – in that crowd of over 500,000 – were wearing black armbands, and it reminded me of Shiva. I was thinking that Shiva would be a cool protest. Imagine the whole country literally sitting for every single person who died in Vietnam. Yeah, Shiva seemed right. Seven days of national mourning for lives lost, lives ruined, families broken. Not supporting or protesting the war. Just mourning the dead. Just sitting.

The next speaker told us protesters had gathered all around the country; in Detroit, Chicago, New York, and San Francisco. All over America, those protesters along with us gathered in DC, the speaker said, stirring up the cheering crowd, would be enough to end the war. He added that no one who fights for his country should come home and have to fight for a job or a roof or for the medical care they need. That also got a big cheer, but I thought it was false hope. Another speaker took over the microphone and Samm said, "Let's walk around."

We made our way through the crowd toward a gathering of tables where suddenly some random guy jumped on a bench and started reading a poem about life after the revolution. Clearly, he felt that he was going to be in charge after the revolution and he was laying out the new rules. The crowd responded to each new proclamation.

"Far out!"

"Tell it, brother!"

We did not join in.

"Am I a traitor if I don't want a revolution?" I asked Samm. I knew about war from the safety of my dinner table, from the living rooms of my parents' friends, from overheard conversations in backyards, and in cars, and at holiday gatherings. Survivors, they called themselves, not victims. They had survived concentration camps. They had survived World War II. They had joined the Resistance. They had escaped capture and death by hiding out in the forests of Europe. They had been taken in by non-Jewish families and raised as Christians. They had evaded the Gestapo in the ghettos. For some, Israel was their gift for having survived. But having a homeland did not come free, and the cost was high as it pitted two occupying groups against each other. I did not need to share their personal experiences to know war was never good.

During the Six-Day War, Ali and I had sat at our dinner table while our parents looked over the latest casualty list of Israelis and tried to figure out how they knew them. There were never more than a few degrees of separation. "Reluctant warriors," my parents called them. Kids barely older than me or Ali. Adults my parents' age, called up from the Reserves. And now, they were driving tanks across the desert. Flying planes into Egypt and Jordan. They were paratroopers crying at the Western Wall. Reciting Kaddish 19 years after the UN declared Jerusalem an international city. Nineteen years after it was seized by Jordan who barred Israelis from entering. Even that moment came with muted celebration. Victory was never free. The cost was lives lost. Lives wasted.

When Israel chose to keep the lands it had seized, my parents were not convinced it would make the nation more secure. They predicted the price of occupation would surely continue to increase as time went on. Just like Lincoln said and Dylan sang, sides could claim to have god on their own side. My money was on any god that may have once cared had long skipped town for a better galaxy.

"No," Samm replied. She was looking at me with her head cocked to one side, waiting for me to come back to her.

I smiled and nodded.

The tables at the Moratorium were littered with newspapers I had never seen before. I eavesdropped on conversations that seemed full of purpose. How could they be so sure, I wondered? I wanted to be sure, too, but I didn't want to be fooled, to be the fool.

Samm and I signed a petition calling for an end to the bombing of Vietnam and another calling for the withdrawal of all US troops from Vietnam. We stood inside the crowd, listening and looking, and I wondered what I would do if I were drafted. Would I take the easy way out and go to Vietnam? Was going along with being drafted easier than not? Would I flee to Canada and never be able to come home again? And not in that Thomas Wolfe way.

Cassius Clay changed his name to Muhammad Ali and refused to join the Army because his religion didn't allow him to kill. Mine also had a commandment against killing. I wasn't sure which religion encouraged it, yet killing went on and on. They took away Muhammad Ali's title and wouldn't let him fight anymore. They took away his livelihood. He paid a steep price.

I wished Joe Namath, Tom Seaver, Willie Mays, everyone would speak out against the war.

Unless they weren't against it. Then I guess I wanted to know that too.

"Look," Samm said, pointing over at the sidewalk.

All along the street, the police kept their view. Barefoot girls went up to them and put flowers in their hats and kissed them and flashed the peace sign. They told them they were not the enemy. It didn't look like they minded the kissing. I agreed that the police were not the opposition and that no one should be fighting with them just because

Congress sent soldiers to Vietnam.

Away from the speakers were small pockets of musicians jamming and small groups promoting their political agendas, recruiting for their part of the cause. It was like they were holding competing demonstrations. These other gatherings just seemed to be having their private party.

Samm needed a bathroom, so we headed to the Smithsonian.

"Isn't it cool that all these places are open and free?" I said.

"This is exactly the stuff we should be spending our collective money on."

"By collective money, you mean taxes?"

"Isn't that the same thing?"

Inside the museum, we checked out the exhibits. The place was mostly empty except for a couple of women showing a little boy the Wright brothers' plane. Samm told me she wasn't a fan of flying.

"I guess we've found a way to make every tool, every invention, every scientific discovery into a weapon," I said.

"Definitely a special human talent," Samm said as we walked away. "We even use music for war."

"The Germans played symphonies as they marched prisoners into the gas chambers," I said.

Suddenly there was a loud noise coming from outside the building.

I wondered if we should stay inside, but Samm was already pulling me along to exit the building and make our way in the direction of the noise, where a large crowd had gathered on Constitution Avenue in front of the Justice Department.

Some guy with a megaphone climbed on top of the Nathan Hale statue and started shouting about pigs and Yippies. He paused, handed off the megaphone, and pulled a small, rectangular card and a lighter from his pocket. He lit the lighter and then lit the card. Taking back his megaphone, he held the burning card in the air, and challenged others to do the same. It worked. I couldn't tell if they were actually their draft cards, but it didn't matter. The point mattered.

And then, almost without being noticed, several vans pulled up onto 10th, and police spilled out onto the street, and it was clear that unlike their fellow officers lining the streets with flowers in their hats, these police – dressed in riot gear – were not likely to interact nicely with the crowd. They formed a line and pulled gas masks over their faces. One of them got up on top of a van and, speaking through a bullhorn, told the crowd to disperse. He said we didn't have a permit and that we needed to vacate the area.

Immediately.

The guy standing on Nathan Hale pulled out a flag and lit it on fire. Then he yelled over and over, "Death to the pig empire."

The crowd joined in with his chant.

The police were not going to like this, I thought. And I was pretty sure the flag- burning guy would be gone the moment the police moved toward the crowd, which they seemed poised and maybe even anxious to do. And then came that moment of stillness, that moment between calm and chaos. The moment between before and after.

"This is not going to turn out well," Samm said. "We should leave."

Maybe there was a signal. I didn't see one. I didn't see who threw the first bottle, but while it sailed toward the line of police, dozens more bottles and rocks quickly took flight. For a moment, I followed their paths through the air. The police didn't wait for the bottles to land. They started marching toward us, swinging their nightsticks and hitting anyone in their way. That was followed by tear gas being propelled into the crowd.

"Let's go." I took hold of Samm's hand, and we tried to weave our way through the crowd.

A canister landed near us and the gas that escaped made it difficult to keep my eyes open. Then, my nose and throat started filling with mucus, making it hard to breathe. As Samm and I made our way through the melee, I noticed that some of the crowd were prepared with gas masks of their own, others had bandanas over their mouths and goggles over their eyes. Someone near us wearing gloves picked up a canister and lobbed it toward the police. I spotted Ali and pulled Samm along as we ran toward her. When we reached her and her friends, a bottle sailed over our heads and shattered on the street.

"You shouldn't be here," Ali said when she saw us. "Come with me," she said as she grabbed our hands. "I'll catch up with you," she yelled to her friends as she pulled us along.

And then, a bottle hit Ali on her head. She released her grip and stumbled as the crowd surged. Samm and I tried to catch her, but the fleeing swarm bumped her out of our reach and she was knocked onto the blacktop. I pushed through to help Ali stand back up. Samm and I locked arms with Ali and the three of us made our escape from the mob. Blood dripped from Ali's scalp.

"I'm okay. Just keep moving," Ali said. "Just get us out of here."

We were back by the reflecting pool when I saw Sunny and Frankie walking toward us. They had spotted us coming, gotten our attention, and were shepherding us to a makeshift medical tent where Sal was handing out canteens and telling people to gargle and spit. I introduced them to Ali and Samm. Sal saw the blood on Ali's head and grabbed some supplies and cleaned her scalp.

"You'll be okay," Frankie told her, then said to the rest of us, "The burning will stop. Don't wipe your eyes. Let them water."

"Dab your eyes gently with this." Sunny handed each of us a cold, damp bandana.

"This won't need stitches," Sal told Ali.

"Who were those people?" I asked Ali. "That sucked."

"Why were you there?" she asked.

"Samm had to pee, so we went to the Smithsonian," I said.

"Don't blame me," Samm said.

"But you knew this was going to happen," I said to Ali. "Why are you involved with those people?"

"It wasn't supposed to go that way," Ali said.

"Are you part of their group?" I asked.

"No. They used us. The organizers came to Columbia and said they were gathering college students together for a teach-in. They lied to us in order to get a crowd. They used us to cause chaos."

"We all use each other," Sal said to no one in particular.

Ali said she wanted to find her friends and see if they were alright. Sal said he'd go with her in case she got dizzy from the blood loss. She said she'd like that.

Before she left, I made her promise to stay away from trouble till we met back at the bus. Sal said he'd make sure of that.

Frankie promised to keep an eye on me and Samm.

I wiped Samm's face. She was very quiet, and I thought she was in shock.

"Are you okay?"

"I'm thinking about my brother."

"Did you think you saw him?"

"This is how he lived in Vietnam. I mean worse, of course, but when he's out in the jungle, this is what he's feeling. That he thought he could die at every moment. He saw so many of his friends die. And I'm sure he killed people. I don't know how he did it. How could he have learned to be part of this? How could he want to go back?"

"These guys were there," I said.

"Is your brother in country?" Frankie asked.

"He just got back from his second tour. He was discharged, but he says he wants to go back," Samm said. "He's against the war, but he says he doesn't know how to be in the world anymore. He wants to go back because he knows how to be over there. I'm not sure I understand."

"We work with guys who have to go back, but who don't want to go back," Sunny said to Samm. "But some of the guys want to – even need to – go back, and we have to be okay with that, too."

"I know. It's just that I worry about him and who he's become. I wonder if I'll recognize him when he comes back. If he comes back," Samm said. Then she turned to me and asked, "How do you know each other?"

"We met at a party," Frankie said.

"Where?"

"It was the party where I met you," I said.

"David was there that night," Samm told Frankie. "David, my brother. I haven't seen him since. I have no idea where he is, or if he's okay."

"Can you ask around, Frankie?" I asked. "You too, Sunny?"

"We can," Frankie said.

"I heard some guys at the party say they would help him get to Vung Tau," I added.

"Vung Tau?" Frankie repeated.

"Yeah, in Vietnam, right?" I asked.

"Shit," Frankie hissed. "That's not what they meant."

"What did they mean?" I asked.

Frankie started asking Samm all sorts of questions about David. Some answers she knew, some she didn't. He told us to hang tight and wait for him.

"Were you scared?" Samm asked me.

"I don't like angry crowds."

"But were you scared that we could get hurt?"

"Sure," I said. "It was crazy. Were you? Were you scared?"

"Yes." Samm was thinking about something. "Did you think we could die?"

"Die? No," I said. "Maimed. Scarred. Blinded. Trampled. Arrested."

"Okay, I get it."

"But not die. No."

Frankie came back with a guy named Cary who had on an army jacket and a purple bandana headband. Cary told us that he was pretty sure he had met Samm's brother.

"Where did you meet him?" Samm asked.

"Back in New York," Cary said. "I think he's still there."

"Where?" Samm asked.

"Vung Tau Base?" I asked.

No one said anything. I looked at Frankie.

"It's a clandestine basecamp some Army bubbas set up in the woods on Ellis Island." Frankie explained.

"It's a real place?" Samm said. "And, Cary, you think David is there?"

"Pretty sure," Cary said. He seemed hesitant to continue.

"They're friendlies," Frankie reassured him.

Cary nodded. "At first, it was just a place for the guys to hang out and get readjusted to being home," he started, "or to be with the only other people who understood what they had gone through...still going through."

"Army guys think of everything," Frankie said. "If Air Force pogues move in, they'll want you to put in a fucking bowling alley."

Cary smiled, and continued. "It kind of grew into a safe house for AWOL guys who didn't want to go – or go back. It was also a sort of underground railroad transfer station for new draft dodgers headed out of the country."

"*Semper Fi*, motherfuckers," Frankie exclaimed, shaking his head.

"Yeah. Some guys are decompressing from their time in Vietnam before they rejoin their friends and family," Cary said. "Some are decomposing – sad and strung out pretty bad. Others don't know how to be back home, and just need a break to escape the pressures of being back in The World for a while. Like R and R. We're there for all of them."

"It's like you're running a halfway house; a two-way, halfway country." Frankie laughed.

I think Samm tensed up when she heard Cary say some of the soldiers were strung out pretty bad. "David doesn't have to go to Canada," Samm said. "He's done. He's been discharged."

"Yeah," Cary said. "He's not going to Canada. But he's thinking about re-enlisting. He's having a hard time being back."

"I hope you're trying to talk him out of it," she said. No one answered her. "Why didn't he tell me where he was?" Samm said to me. She was crying. I put my arm around her. She kept her eyes on Cary.

"He's probably trying to protect you," Cary said.

"From what?"

"From him. Till he's better. Till he can handle being back home."

"But I can help him," Samm said.

"It's not that simple," Sunny said. I had forgotten she was there.

"I'm his sister."

"That's not always enough," Sunny added. "It helps. It definitely helps. But it's not always enough."

"I want to see him. I need to leave now and find him and tell him he can come home. I need to know he's okay." Samm turned to Frankie. "How do I get to Vung…to the base camp?"

"When I get back to New York, I can get a message to your brother and let him know you want to see him," Cary said.

"I'm not waiting. I'm going to find him." Samm let go of my hand. "Zach, I'll see you back in New York. I need to leave. Now." Samm started walking away and almost immediately started to jog.

"What are you doing?" Frankie said, tapping my shoulder. "Go get her. She'll never find him. We'll take her."

"We will?" Cary asked.

"Yes." Frankie said. "We will. Tonight."

I ran after Samm. "Did you think I wouldn't go with you?" I said, catching up to her.

"It's not your problem."

"You could at least give me a chance to say no."

"He's my brother."

"And you're my girl. Which means I'm going with you."

"I'm your girl?"

"Yes. Now please, can we stop running."

"When did you decide?" Samm said, stopping.

"That I'm coming with you?"

"That I'm your girl."

"I don't know. I just did."

"And I don't have a say in that?" Samm said. "You just decided."

"Aren't you?"

"Was it the sex?"

"No. Before that," I said. "After Washington Square. That night I saw you play."

"How did you know I'm your girl?"

"I just knew."

"But how? How did you know?" Samm asked.

"When I went home and I realized that you make me happy when I am with you and that I missed you when I wasn't with you."

"Okay."

"Okay?"

"Yes."

"Okay, you're my girl?"

"Yes."

"Can we go back and let Frankie help us find your brother?"

"Because I'm your girl?" Samm said.

"Because we need him to find David," I said. "And yes, because you're my girl." I liked the way that sounded. I took her hand as we turned and walked back together.

"We'll find him," Sunny said, hugging Samm when she saw us.

Ali and Sal were back and they had Jonah and Lu with them.

"Look who we found," Ali said.

I was relieved at not having to try and find Jonah and Lu in the crowd. I told them all the new change in plans, and Ali smiled.

"Who's in?" Cary said. "Plenty of room in the van."

"I'm coming with you," Ali said. "They won't miss me on the bus."

"Yeah, she's coming with us," Sal laughed. "We need to get your sister out of DC before she causes a major riot." Ali laughed too, like Sal was telling an inside joke. She looked happy. I wasn't used to seeing her happy.

"We arrived together, we leave together," Jonah said.

"Let's roll," Lu added.

"What did you do?" I asked Ali as Cary pulled up with the van. She simply shook her head and her smile turned into a thoughtful secret across her face.

"He was suicidal," Samm said to Sunny as she stepped into the van. "The last time I saw him. He said he wanted to die."

SOUNDS OF SILENCE

"I know a route to Canada," I announced as Cary turned the van onto New York Avenue.

"Say what?" Frankie said.

"I know a route using only backroads that leads to a place where we can cross the border without having to pass through any checkpoints."

"Okay," Frankie said. "First, that's a little bit cool. Second, that's so completely random and totally strange. Plus, we're only going to Manhattan."

"If you needed to get draft evaders safely out of the US," I said. "I could do it."

"Something is extremely wrong with you," Frankie laughed.

"Hey, Frankie," Jonah said, "you also said that the first time you met Zach. Man, you were right then, and you've even more right now."

"So hurtful," I said to Jonah. "Why so hurtful?"

"Seriously," Ali laughed, "that's fucking peculiar. Even for you, Zach."

"I like maps."

"Why would you know how to sneak into Canada," Samm asked me. "Are you planning a trip?"

"That's the thing," Jonah said. "He's not so much sneaking into Canada as slipping out of the US."

"Yeah," Ali said. "That clears everything up."

"You knew about this?" Lu asked Jonah.

Jonah laughed. "I found all these maps in his room. In back of his albums. That's when he told me that he had joined Triple A so he could map out an escape route for when the US decides to start rounding up Jews. Weird for some people but not for Zach"

"What makes you think that Canada would harbor Jews?" Ali said.

"Nothing," I said. "But they're close. And they take draft evaders."

"You joined the Triple A in order to study their maps and plot the best route?" Samm asked.

"More or less," I said.

"Far out," Cary laughed. "We have a card-carrying member of Triple A in our midst. I, myself, am a member of double A. As in A-A."

Cary was a funny guy. And a good driver. He served in Vietnam. Army. Two tours. When he returned to the world in 1967 he joined up with Vietnam Veterans Against the War.

"The thing is," Jonah said," Zach's dad is in a wheelchair. There is an added degree of difficulty."

"Is your dad a vet?" Sal asked Ali.

"Polio," she said.

"And you think you're responsible for getting your family out?" Samm said. "All by yourself?"

"That's a heavy burden, man," Frankie said.

"Too heavy," Sal added.

"He ain't heavy, he's my brother," Ali said quietly. She squeezed my hand.

"It's sweet," Sunny said, looking at me.

"Is this because of Grandma and Grandpa's passports?" Ali asked me.

"Not just that," I said. I needed to change the conversation, so I asked Sal what kind of trouble Ali caused. He was happy to tell and Ali looked happy to listen to him talk about her.

"You should have been there," Sal said. "You would have enjoyed it. All of you should have been there."

"It was nothing," Ali said.

"It was not nothing," Sal said. "So, Ali is looking for her friends from Columbia who were at the Justice Department. We were over by all those alphabet signs. SDS, PL, YSA, SWP, YAWF. Some others. Doesn't matter. Suddenly she just bolts, and I hurry to catch up and follow her. I was worried she might have a concussion."

"I saw that asshole from Hopkins," Ali said, "the one who lied to get us to show up for what was supposed to be a teach-in."

"This dude," Sal continued, "he sees her coming and acts like he was expecting her and he handed her a notebook telling her she's just in time for their meeting and she should take notes. I can see he's clueless. I can see Ali is pissed. I mean, anyone could see she was pissed."

"She doesn't hide it well," I said.

"No, she does not," Sal said. "So then, Ali threw the notebook back at him and told him he was a fraud and a coward." Sal paused.

I looked at Samm, and she seemed to be enjoying the distraction.

"It was a beautiful thing." Sal went on to tell us how a crowd gathered and Clueless Guy should have just walked away. "Instead, this dude says, who the hell is this bitch? And then he added that someone needed to take Ali into the tent and fuck her so she'd calm the hell down. And now I'm not laughing anymore," Sal said.

Ali was smiling and looking at Sal.

"What happened," Sal continued, "was that these chicks, like five or six of them, they come and stand next to Ali and they do not look happy at all. This one Spanish chick, she gets right up in Clueless Dude's face and calmly offers to cut his dick off and shove it in his mouth. That did the trick, and he turned and walked away. I don't think he wanted to find out if she was serious. So Spanish Chick raises her fist and yells 'Power to the Sisterhood,' and gives Ali a big hug."

"Sisterhood indeed," Lu echoed, and we all laughed.

"I think Sal was angrier than I was," Ali said.

Frankie lit a joint and Sunny found some music on the radio. A college station out of Baltimore was playing "Aquarius," and I was thinking that it would be cool if peace could guide the planets and love could steer the stars. But here on Earth there had always been endless fighting and killing no matter which way the planets were aligned.

I might have said so. I might have mentioned this to everyone, but Lu started singing along. So did Sunny and Cary. I stopped thinking and joined the singing, Frankie turned up the volume, and we sang as loud as we could because who wouldn't want to be part of the dawning of a new age. I mean the old age, or whatever it was called, wasn't doing so well, so time to move on and start again.

I put my arm around Samm, and we smiled at each other as we sang and the music gave us a break. Nothing else mattered while we sang and love was fueling the van and harmony was all around and I was with people I liked and who liked me and I was grateful to have reached that moment together with each of them.

Later, when we crossed into Jersey, Frankie turned to me and said, "You do understand that most of the guys helping draftees get out of the US and into Canada are like special ops guys. Green Berets, SEALs, Rangers, those guys. They can get in and out of anywhere unnoticed. Five of them are in the van with us right now and you can't see them," he laughed. "Pretty sure they can read maps, too. A lot of us can, you know."

When we came out of the Holland Tunnel, Sal took out one of those portable radios the Army used. He got someone on the other end and told them that he had a group and we needed to get picked up. I noticed that he didn't tell them where to meet us. Cary turned the van down Houston Street, and we listened to folks on WBAI offer their thoughts and analysis about what the events that took place that day in DC meant to the anti-war effort. They seemed certain that opposition against the war had overtaken support for the war. Disapproval had reached a critical mass and its voice was loud and unified.

The sun was setting and the air was cooling with a November chill when Cary pulled the van over at South Cove near Battery Park. We exited the van and followed Frankie through the park, which was mostly empty.

Lu put her arm around Samm and asked how she was doing. I put my hand on Jonah's shoulder and told him I was glad he had come along and how cool it was that we were here together. Ali came up behind us and kissed each of our cheeks and told us she was proud of us.

Sal told us to wait with him as Cary and Frankie went ahead to talk to three guys who were hanging around near a bench. They kind of looked like they were homeless. Sunny told us there were always a few vets on that bench.

"They keep people away from the docking area," Sunny said.

"What docking area?" Ali asked.

Cary waved us over, and Frankie led us through some bushes and onto a trail that took us to the water's edge where a boat was waiting. Once we were all on board, the coxswain maneuvered away from the shore before turning on lights. As we made our way toward Ellis Island, I turned to look back at the Manhattan skyline which was even more outstanding from a small boat in the Hudson River. In front of us, the Statue of Liberty's torch glowed in the evening sky. The air was breezy, but the sea was calm that night and uncrowded. I was trying to find a traffic pattern that the handful of boats and ships navigating the waters of New York seemed to be following. Off to our left, the Staten Island Ferry was heading back to Manhattan. On our boat, no one was talking. Maybe it was the cold air that had us huddled together. Or maybe it was that we remembered why we were there and that we had no idea what to expect or what we would encounter when we went ashore.

The skipper radioed ahead and then shut the lights. We drifted for a few moments and then turned into some brush that gave way easily. On the other side, we maneuvered along the dock where several men were waiting for us. They tied the boat and helped us onto the platform.

"You have to stay calm when we walk through camp," Frankie said.

"Okay," Jonah said.

"Why will we need to stay calm?" Lu asked. "What will make us not calm?"

"The place can appear a bit unusual," Frankie said. "It might seem rough, to outsiders. Or chaotic. You will think it is a squatters camp, but it isn't," he added.

"It's home to these guys and they are comfortable here," Cary said.

"But not all of them trust outsiders," Sal said. "Stay close to us."

"It's a safe place for them," Sunny said. "And you'll be safe here as well."

"And this is mainly for you, Zach," Frankie said. "You know how I love that you're curious about shit. But here, for now, at least for this visit, no questions. No interviews. We're here to find David."

"You're listening," Jonah said to me.

"I got it," I said. "No questions."

"Cool," Frankie said.

"See, I didn't even ask you why."

"He must really like you," Jonah said to Samm.

The smell of pot was everywhere. That same camel shit smell from when Jonah and I first met Frankie and Sal and Sunny. There were several maps of Vietnam with colored pins in them. I didn't ask what the pins were. I was afraid the answer would involve casualties and death. But maybe it was where they had been. Which would also mean casualties and death. The tents formed a perimeter and they were covered with graffiti.

Viet Nam, Love It Or Leave It.

Gulf of Tonkin Cruise Line.

Nothing Is True – Everything Is Permitted.

Flower Power.

Ali put her arm through mine and let us fall to the back of the group. "You did good," she whispered in my ear. "She's so strong. I love when women own their woman power and she does." She kissed my cheek.

"I have no idea what you're talking about," I told her. "But if you're saying she's awesome, I agree with you. I'm lucky she likes me."

"So lucky."

We passed an empty tent with a ping pong table. Another tent had a white square with a red cross that must have been used as their medical tent, and I thought I recognized the nurse who helped me and Jonah that time we got beat up in the park. But I couldn't stop to see for sure. We were looking for David, and Cary had told us to stay together.

The place looked like part hippie commune, part military base, part summer camp. But its feel was all military base. It wasn't like anyone saluted or anything. And except for some hats and jackets, no one was dressed in their fatigues. Plus, most of the guys had long hair. And then I realized what was missing. There were hardly any women. And we had four in our group.

I stopped in front of a small improvised greenhouse. Frankie came over and told me it was what I thought it was. A bit of Vietnam agriculture. Pastures of plenty. A peace garden of sorts with Vietnamese seeds planted in US soil. He said he'd give me a tour another time, but we needed to keep moving.

Within the tent formation, in the middle of the camp, some guys were sitting around two fire pits and four wooden tables. Some were actively doing nothing. Others were playing cards or chess or checkers. Running through the quad was a waist-high wall made of sandbags. The wall was not straight or uniform. Instead, it meandered and roamed, following a random and likely meaningless longitudinal and latitude markings. Back in Vietnam, walls like this were used as fortifications and shelter. They might mean the difference between life and death.

"What's the wall for?" I asked Frankie.

"Here, the wall simply is," he said. "It doesn't need a strategic or pragmatic purpose. Maybe it's nostalgic. Maybe therapeutic. Maybe it's simply meant to be sat on and leaned against. Because here in The World, that object that may have been a thin line between life and death over there is just a bag of sand."

On one side of the wall was a Christmas tree and next to it a Menorah.

"What's the deal with the oil and Hanukkah," Sal asked Ali.

Ali looked at me. "You're on."

"It's not really about one day's oil lighting the temple for eight days. It's about lighting up the dark and remembering that a small band of Jewish resistance fighters, possibly the first people to use guerrilla warfare, took on a larger and more powerful Greek army who were trying to force them to worship Greek gods."

"Sounds a lot like Vietnam."

"Too much," Cary said.

"The Jews persevered?"

"Outlasted the Greeks."

"Sounds exactly like Vietnam."

"What's that thing Twain said?" Ali asked. "History may not repeat itself, but it certainly rhymes."

"Abso-fucking-lutely," Sal said.

I heard Marvin Gaye through a nearby tent singing that men weren't supposed to cry, but cry he did. And then I noticed that Samm was carefully making her way toward a guy sitting on the sandbag wall. He had his back to us and was playing guitar and singing "Blackbird." It was one of Samm's favorite songs, and I had heard her play it on her cello in Washington Square. I made my way over to Samm and stood behind her. His voice was haunting and a bit pleading. Like he was hoping that every person in camp would mend their broken wings and find their moment to be free. I'd only met David once, and he had been on my back for most of the meeting, but it was clear from the look on Samm's face as she listened that she, that we, had found David.

When the song ended, he stopped playing and turned around. Neither Samm or David spoke. He had a beard now and he stared at Samm from behind sunglasses. After several long moments, he started playing again. This time he sang that Sam Cooke song about change coming. On cue, Samm joined in. She rarely sang when she played cello, and that was a pity because she was good. Samm and David harmonized about that long wait for change to show up, about how, despite life being overwhelmingly difficult and almost too much to bear, death with all its unknown was far more frightening. They sang on, becoming more mournful. Resigned to get knocked down again and promising to get back up again. Yeah, change was going to come, the song promised. It was inevitable. I thought it had already arrived.

When they were done singing, David looked up. "Hi, Samm."

"Hello, David," Samm said.

"Why are you here?" David asked.

"To see you," Samm said.

"Okay," David said.

"How are you?" Samm asked.

"I don't know."

"Will you come home?" Samm asked.

"I am home."

"To see Mom and Dad. They are worried about you. They miss you. I miss you."

"I can't leave. It's not safe for me out there."

"You're safe with us. We're your family. We'll take care of you," Samm said.

"These are my brothers. We take care of each other."

"Then come home for a visit."

"You might not be safe with me."

"Is that what you're worried about?" Samm sat next to David.

"I'm tired of the body counts. I am tired of the bleeding that doesn't stop. I am tired," David said. "I am very tired and I am tired of being tired."

"Then come home and rest."

"There is no rest."

In the end, David was not willing to leave, but we had to. The best Samm could do was get David to promise to think about coming home for Christmas.

"I need a miracle," David said as we left. "But there are no miracles. If there ever were any, they are all gone. Used up. Every one of them."

Samm cried.

• • •

A couple of weeks later, on the first of December, with the demonstration in DC and finding David on Ellis Island still fresh in our memory, Jonah came over to watch the Selective Service draft lottery drawing being broadcast live on TV.

My father said he thought this would help the country decide if it wanted to keep fighting in Vietnam. He said that since everyone in Israel, every man and every woman, had to serve in the army, politicians were more hesitant to send their citizens to war.

It was a Monday night and we watched "Mayberry RFD" until CBS interrupted the show with Roger Mudd who spoke to us in a hushed voice from inside the Selective Service National Headquarters in Washington, DC. I wasn't sure if he was afraid to disturb the ceremony or wanted to accentuate the gravity of the occasion. He announced that this was the first time in 27 years that the United States held a draft lottery. Then, he pointed to the large glass container filled with 366 blue plastic balls, each ball had a calendar date printed on it, each ball held many a young man's destiny. The balls were removed by hand, one at a time, read aloud, and then added to a list till all the days of the calendar were filled in. Even though we were too young, we felt the tension of knowing every ball drawn would change lives.

I pulled out my little notebook and wrote down each of our birthdays, even though we were not old enough to be drafted. The first ball drawn was September 14. Every man born on September 14 in the years between 1944 and 1950 was assigned lottery number 1.

We had been curious about which one of us would have their birthday come up first. Samm was. Did she win? September 6, was picked 6th. I entered that in my notebook.

Jonah was next, the 21st pick, August 10.

"That's good, Jonah," my father said.

"Why?" Jonah asked.

"Because it's good to use up your low numbers when they don't count. It increased the probability of getting a high number in the future."

I knew that he was wrong about the probability, but I liked that he said it.

Next up was Mel, who was 148th, April 16.

It took a while till I followed Mel at 202. It was like being welcomed into a club that should not exist. And unlike Jonah, I did not use up a low number.

Next pick was Lu at 205, February 27.

Ali was number 257, September 28.

Tony was the big winner, coming in last at 305, January 1.

The drawing continued until all days of the year had been paired with sequence numbers.

I spoke to Ali the next day and she said guys who got winning numbers were over at the administration building that morning. They were there to withdraw from school, she said. Some were talking about enlisting. Some were talking about going to Canada. Others stood waiting in silence. I was thinking that statistically, several of them would die in Vietnam before I finished high school.

Later that day, my English teacher had us read Shirley Jackson's, "The Lottery." Talk about insanity. A lottery where winning is losing. Seriously, how dumb were those townsfolk? My teacher said the story was on our statewide year-end Regents Exam, and, she added, the timing had nothing to do with the draft.

When I called Samm to make plans for the weekend she was all excited because David told her he was ready to come home for a visit. She asked me to come along with her to South Cove to meet him. She said she didn't want to be alone if he didn't show. I wondered if she was also afraid to be alone with him if he did.

That Sunday, I met Samm inside the Times Square Station where we grabbed a newspaper and caught the 1 train downtown. We found seats and read about the chaos at the Rolling Stones concert the night before. For the last stop on their tour, The Rolling Stones organized a free concert at the Altamont Speedway, which they said was their California Woodstock.

"It would be cool to live in California," I said.

"Listen to this line-up," Samm said. "Santana, Jefferson Airplane, Crosby, Stills, Nash and Young, and The Grateful Dead. But The Dead left without playing after the Airplane's Marty Balin got knocked out in a fight while he was on stage."

"What?"

"In the middle of his performance."

"What else does it say?"

"With the Stones on stage, a guy waving a gun was stabbed by one of the Hells Angels who was acting as Security for the band. The guy died. That sucks."

"What the hell. This is rock and roll. It's supposed to be all about the music and peace and love. This is not Woodstock."

"David was going to be a musician," Samm said. "We were going to play together. He lost that in Vietnam. It was his whole life. I'm not sure what is left to his life. I'm glad you heard him play at that camp."

"It probably wasn't his whole life, and his life is not over. And your life with him isn't either."

"But it's not the same."

"No. It's not." I put my arm around Samm. "It's not. I wish I could say differently, but it's not. And it might never be. But it's not over."

We left the paper on the seat for someone else to read and made our way to South Cove where David was waiting for us. He had a small backpack slung over his shoulder. He was wearing his USMC field jacket and carrying his guitar. He looked happy. I'd never seen Samm so nervous. David said he wanted to see the tree at Rockefeller Center, so that's what we wanted to do.

We checked out the tree and watched the ice skaters for a while. I got us all some roasted chestnuts to share and we found a bench.

"I'm boring now, but I used to be interesting," David said. I think he was saying it to me.

"Let's play some carols," Samm said. "It will be fun." She removed his guitar and placed the case in front of them to collect money. That made them look legit.

They opened with "Jingle Bells" which attracted a crowd. They were good. Really good. Then they went from "Ave Maria" to "Silent Night". They knew how to harmonize, and it didn't hurt that Samm was beautiful, and David could play, and they both could sing. They sang like they were singing for everyone who couldn't. For the weak and the voiceless. For the children and the soldiers. For those who wanted to sing, but were told they shouldn't. For those who were afraid to sing.

It was outstanding.

While the crowd applauded, Samm leaned over and whispered in David's ear, and he smiled. Samm announced that the next song was for me, and they did the dreidel song. I laughed and others clapped. Hanukkah had started, and Samm knew her audience.

When the song was over, Samm announced that their last song was "White Christmas" which brought loud applause, a larger crowd, and a bunch more money. Funny that it was written by a Jew. A lot of great Christmas songs were written by Jews. I had to wonder why there weren't any good Hanukkah songs.

An older man in a suit walked over to David while he tuned his guitar. He looked right at David and said, "Semper Fi," then leaned over and placed some bills in the guitar case.

David jumped up and responded, "OORAH." The guy saluted David, turned, and left.

Samm started in on "White Christmas," and David sat back down and joined her, and together they sang about snow and sleighs and bells and treetops.

David packed his guitar and asked Samm if she minded walking home. He wanted to give the money to some homeless vets in Central Park. He also asked Samm to help him pick out some Christmas presents for their parents. I left them at Times Square and made my way to the subway where I descended the stairs into the tunnel that would take me back to Queens.

When I next spoke to Samm that evening, she said David had agreed to join their parents and see her play during the holiday concert at her school. I was studying for finals and we made plans for me and Jonah and Lu, the Jews, to come over to her house on Christmas Day.

On Christmas Eve, I went with my parents to have Chinese food. This completely arbitrary and absurd custom, this unwritten agreement between Chinese restaurants and Jews, seemed somewhat obligatory. If they stayed open, we should come. Since my family hardly ever went out to eat, this Christmas Eve tradition was like a mini-holiday for us. After dinner, I met Jonah, and we went to see *They Shoot Horses, Don't They?* and officially kicked off our school vacation.

The next day, Jonah and Lu and I went to Samm's house to spend the day hanging out in Manhattan. Tony and Mel were spending the day with their families.

"You're giving Samm a Christmas present?" Jonah said.

"Yup," I said as we walked up Columbus Avenue.

"Is she giving you one?"

"I don't know," I said. "We didn't talk about exchanging gifts."

"Would that be weird if she did?" Lu said. "Shouldn't she give you a Hanukkah present?"

"We don't do Hanukkah presents," I said.

"We do," Lu said. "It's great for me because my folks were so worried about me liking Christmas back in Nashville, where it's a big thing."

"It's a big thing here too," Jonah said.

"Yeah, but there are hardly any Jews in Nashville, so they went all out. They don't want me wishing we celebrated Christmas, so they competed to win with Christmas shopping. Which means I win. Not like I'd convert for the presents."

"Yeah," Jonah said. "My parents go all out, too. Every year I get socks. This year they threw in underwear."

"You have new undies?" Lu said. "I can't wait."

"And now, I can't wait," Jonah said.

"I guess if I celebrated Hanukkah that way and got her a Hanukkah gift, then sure, she should give me a gift on Hanukkah. But she invited me for Christmas morning and it's her holiday."

"Plus," Lu said, "she's cute."

"Very," I laughed.

"And let's not forget that she's willing to have sex with you," Jonah laughed.

"That's what I'm saying," I said.

Samm answered the intercom.

"The Jews have arrived," Lu said to Samm from the lobby.

Samm buzzed us in, and we took the elevator up to her apartment.

Samm's mom opened the door and led us into the living room where Samm and David were playing music. They were wearing matching long stocking caps, and I felt like I was in a Christmas play. There was a pile, a very large pile, of wrapping paper and opened presents in front of the tree. My present suddenly seemed lame, so I stuck it back in my jacket pocket.

We were offered eggnog, and while Samm's mom served it, her dad warned us that there was a drop of alcohol in it. I thought he was trying to be a responsible parent or that maybe, because he was a lawyer, he felt the need to warn us. But after I took a sip of the eggnog, I realized that he was drunk, and that Samm's mom was also. Samm and David were probably drunk, too. And there was a lot more than a drop of rum in the eggnog. I think the ratio of alcohol to nog was tipped in favor of the rum.

I looked at Samm, who smiled at me as she played. Lu lifted her glass and toasted our hosts, followed by Jonah who toasted Christmas and the birth of Baby Jesus. Samm's mom filled our glasses, which were only half empty, and we did our best to catch up.

Later, in Samm's room, I mentioned that I had a small Christmas present, and added, "I wasn't sure if you wanted a present."

"Why would I not want a present? Did you see our tree? We do presents big. Lots of presents."

"Yeah, that was a lot of presents," I said. "But, from me. I just wasn't sure if you and I do Christmas presents."

"Because you're Jewish?"

"Well, that too," I said. "I never got anyone a Christmas present before."

"My own little Christmas virgin," she said.

"That's funny. Are you done?"

"Not if you keep making it that easy for me."

"Anyway, do we do Christmas?" I said.

"I did not get you anything."

"Okay."

"But that should not stop you from giving me a present." Samm put out her hands. "Do you have it with you?"

"I do."

"Hand it over."

I removed her present from my jacket and she started tearing the paper off before I let go of it.

"Careful," I said. "It's delicate."

Samm didn't say anything at first. She just stared at the cover of the hardback edition of *On The Road*. She looked at me and opened the book and carefully turned the first couple of pages, stopping when she saw it was signed by Jack Kerouac. She traced the signature and then closed the book and held it tight against her chest. She still didn't say a thing.

"It's wrong for a Christmas present, right?" I asked.

Samm didn't say a thing. A tear came out of her left eye.

"It's more like a Hanukkah gift?" I said. "How about it's just something from me to you. We don't have to make a big deal out of it."

"Stop talking."

"Okay," I said. "Why?"

"It's perfect. It's the best present ever."

And then I had nothing to say, and we went back into the living room where Jonah told Samm we got tickets for everyone to see Jimi Hendrix on New Year's Eve at the Fillmore.

"Hendrix," Samm said. "Cool."

"Plus, it's New Years," I said.

"Yeah, that part. I never understood. I don't see why it's a big deal." Samm said.

"I know, but it's our first it-doesn't-mean-anything-New-Year's-Eve celebration together," I said. "And it's Hendrix. So not completely without meaning."

"Okay," Samm said. "I'll give you the Hendrix part."

"The calendar is going to change from the Sixties to the Seventies," Jonah said. "That's pretty cool."

"There's something about an ending and a beginning that seems to mean something," Lu said.

"A toast," I said, raising my eggnog, "to closing out the year and decade at the Fillmore listening to Jimi Hendrix together, all of us, together."

"I predict that 1970 is going to be a good year for us," Jonah said. "1969 was good and it got us ready for an even better 1970."

"You're kind of sentimental," Lu laughed.

"You're making fun of me?" Jonah said.

"She is," Samm said. "And I approve."

"But you'll both still go with us to see Hendrix."

"Like you said," Samm smiled. "It's Hendrix."

"And we'll all be together," I repeated.

Sure, I knew the Sixties weren't over at midnight. I was not attached to anniversaries that were only celebrated in multiples of five any more than the anniversary of waking up each day, or being alive each moment. Still, pausing to notice change seemed like a good habit.

And really, what was wrong with hoping a change was going to come?

PLAY WITH FIRE

"It's too fucking cold," Jonah said, as we rode the subway to the Filmore.

"January first is the wrong time to turn the calendar over," Lu said.

"It's not cold everywhere in January," Mel said.

"It's not even a new season. It's not a harvest," Lu said.

"You seem to hate January," Tony said.

"There's nothing special about January," Lu said. "Except that it's cold."

"Nothing," Tony said. "Not even my January birthday."

"Okay, that was a fucking set up," Lu laughed. "I stand corrected. There is one special moment in January. But you better be throwing a hell of a birthday bash and you best be inviting me."

"Doesn't matter when the calendar turns over," Samm said, "New Year's brings no particular resolution to anything. It offers no beginning. No end. Not for the year and not for the decade. It's totally arbitrary.

"The week, though, that's a brilliant invention," I said. "That marks the hell out of stuff. The week is tough. It takes control of time."

"Okay kids, enough babble," Tony said. "Tonight, while in the company of you three fine women, we will get to listen to Jimi Hendrix do his thing while he plays us out of the Sixties and into the Seventies. Does it mean anything? Who cares? I do not give a fuck either way. It is a great excuse for the world to throw a party, and I am always in favor of parties." With that, he kissed Mel.

"Now that is something I can get behind," Lu said, kissing Jonah.

When we emerged onto Astor Place and headed east and then down Second Avenue toward the Fillmore where we joined hundreds of other freezing folks waiting to enter the hall. The sidewalk around us was noisy with chatter, and people spilled onto the avenue which hummed with the sounds of traffic. The crowd stretched around the corner onto 6th Street. We hugged our girls for warmth.

Loud cheers erupted as the doors were opened, and the crowd quickly surged toward the promise of warmth. We found our seats and left our jackets on. Tony lit a joint and we waited for our bodies to thaw and our minds to forget we were cold.

When Jimi Hendrix took the stage, he introduced Billy Cox on bass, and Buddy Miles on drums and told us that they were the Band of Gypsys. At one point they played a song called "Machine Gun." Hendrix dedicated it to soldiers everywhere, in Chicago, in New York, and the ones who were fighting over in Vietnam. In the middle of the song, Hendrix went off on a long solo that was truly outstanding. I'd never heard anything like it. Never. Not even close.

Samm told me that she wished she could play cello like Hendrix played guitar.

"You, do," I said. "Every time I've ever heard you play."

"What do you think about when you hear him play like that?" she asked me.

"Like when you play that Bach song or that time on the subway when I read Kerouac," I said. "It's like when we have sex. I'm thinking, but not thinking."

The Gypsys said good night, wished us all a happy New Year, and hoped we each had a million more of them. We were the early show that night – the next show would actually start in 1969 and end in

1970, but we couldn't get tickets for that.

Houston Street was buzzing as we emerged from the concert. We tried to stay warm as we ran across the wide street to Katz's Deli where they let us order wine with our sandwiches.

"To this moment," Jonah said, raising his glass.

"A thousand thousands," Lu said.

"As long as there's meat on the shin of a sparrow we will all live long and prosper," Tony said.

At first no one responded as we tried to figure out what he had just said. Then we laughed and drank up. We ordered more wine and toasted Hendrix, the three girls, the Mets, diners, pot, and anything we could think of till we ran out of wine. When more wine came we toasted the wine. As midnight approached, the deli counted down together and when the clock changed, we kissed, and said goodbye to the Sixties, and then goodbye to Katz's.

Samm's parents told us that we could all stay over after the concert and we headed uptown. Samm was looking forward to getting home and all of us hanging out with David. She wouldn't say, but I think she was hoping that the new decade would somehow allow him to have a fresh start, a clean break from his past.

Once uptown, we climbed the subway stairs to the street and turned left onto 73rd Street and stopped. A police car and ambulance were blocking the street with their lights flashing.

"That's my building," Samm said. She took off running, and I followed.

"That can't be good," Jonah said, running alongside me.

The building's front door was open and we ran up the stairwell to Samm's apartment. Her front door was wide open, too. Samm ran inside calling for David. Jonah and I followed her into the living room where the Christmas tree still stood. Samm disappeared down the hallway, but we stood waiting in the living room. Tony and Lu and Mel came in and waited with us. We listened to soft spoken voices, but none of us could make out what was being said.

I heard Samm crying. Jonah shoved me toward the hallway, and I saw Samm coming toward me.

"He's gone." She leaned into me and buried her face in my shoulder.

"Who?"

"David."

"You mean he left?"

"He's dead," she said. "He's dead."

"What?"

"He's dead."

"I don't understand."

Two medics wheeled a stretcher into the living room. David was on the stretcher with a sheet covering him. Samm's parents were holding onto one side of the stretcher. They were going to go with David in the ambulance and asked us to stay behind with Samm.

Samm let go of me and stopped the medics so she could take David's hand in hers. She leaned over, pulled back the sheet, and kissed his face. I'd never seen a dead person. He looked so normal. Like he was resting.

When they were gone, Samm showed us David's note. I read it and passed it to Jonah.

I'm sorry to put you through this. The thing that kept me going till now was to avoid putting all of you through this. But I can't go on any longer. I can not live with myself and the things I know and the things I've seen and the things I've done. I am tired of remembering because it's the same as reliving and I can no longer go on reliving what I remember.

I love all of you and don't want to do this to you. It may not seem that way right now, but I know that your lives will be easier without me. I am glad we had these last few days together and I hope you know how much I love each of you and I am sorry for the pain I caused you.

David had certainly seen more than his share of death up close. He had carried many of his dead brothers across fields and landing zones to get their bodies home – often while risking his own safety. And he had carried them with him every day. He hadn't been capable of letting them go. Maybe he was unwilling.

And here he was, at peace, finally. That was what he sought, that was what he wanted for his family. For his fellow vets. For his country. For Vietnam.

III

1970

GIMME SHELTER

Samm suggested that David would want to be buried with his brothers in the military graveyard on Long Island, but her parents insisted he be buried with the rest of their family in the Bronx. They wanted him closer and to be able to visit him more often. I think they also wanted to end up together with him. Later. But they had no problem with Samm asking some of David's military buddies to come to the funeral. In fact, they seemed pleased when Samm suggested Marines as pallbearers. They didn't ask Samm how she knew Marines who knew David.

On Friday, I met up with Samm, and we took the subway downtown to see Frankie and Sal who lived in Alphabet City. Ali had been hanging out there with Sal and I was looking forward to seeing her, though I felt bad about looking forward to anything.

We got off at West 4th because Samm wanted to walk through Washington Square. We stopped to listen to a blues guitarist, but Samm wasn't paying him any attention. She seemed to be searching for someone or something. I asked her if she was looking for Freddie, but she said she wasn't.

We left the park and headed east toward St. Marks Place.

"Don't you guys spend like seven days not listening to music?" Samm asked me.

"The idea is to reflect on the person who died and about life and death. We're not supposed to think about ourselves."

Sunny opened the door and led us into the kitchen where she was making pancakes. Frankie joined us, and we sat so he could ask Samm questions and take notes about the funeral.

"They'll be there," Frankie said. "His brothers will carry him."

CCR was playing from somewhere in the apartment. A door opened and the music got louder, and then Sal and Ali appeared in the kitchen.

Frankie filled them in and we had some coffee together. Then Frankie and Sal and Ali and Sunny left to locate pallbearers.

David's body went on display at the funeral home on Saturday. This was Samm's family's way of letting friends and relatives say goodbye. A different religion, an alternative custom, another ritual. Another version to help the living keep living. I'm not sure any of them work. But they all work.

The next day, Jonah, Lu, Tony, Mel, and I took the subway in to meet Samm at her church. When we got there, six Marines in dress blues were standing at the top of the steps in front of the open doors. They were the pallbearers Frankie and Sal had promised.

Inside, filling most of the back ten or so rows, were about 100 vets, men and women from all the branches, in various attire. I saw Cary, and he came over and hugged me and walked away without saying a thing.

We moved toward the front of the sanctuary where the casket was on display. Ali was walking toward us and she gave me a long hug before leading us to a row of seats with Frankie, Sunny, and Sal. Samm was sitting between her parents in the front row.

Samm was there to bury her brother, and I was sitting with my sister and my friends.

"She's Episcopalian," Tony told me. "Samm is Episcopalian."

"She told me that a while ago," I said. "Not sure what that is. She's still Christian, right?"

"According to my family, an Episcopalian is a Catholic who failed Latin."

"I don't get it," I said.

"Yeah," Tony said. "Neither do I. None of us know Latin. But Catholics think that's very funny."

"Maybe I shouldn't tell that one to Samm's parents," I said.

"Yeah, probably not," Tony said. "At least not for a few days."

The priest spoke about better places and rebirth and god's plan and stuff that was hard to listen to. It was like David was being welcomed into a club of the dead, and the priest was trying to justify, to rationalize, to normalize the membership fees as he claimed things happened for a reason. Which meant he claimed to know for sure that things happened for a reason. His whole sermon, his act, it wasn't working. Two things were wrong. One, you had to think there's a god. You had to believe it. And two, you had to have faith that that god gave a shit about David.

David was young and had been sent to war, and even though he survived Vietnam it still killed him. Samm lost a brother. Her parents lost a son. There was simply no sense to be made, and the priest's attempt to do so seemed artificial and a little insulting.

It made no sense. Non-sense.

After the priest was done, Samm stood and climbed the steps onto the stage. She placed some papers on the pulpit and told us she was reading from Walt Whitman.

"I celebrate myself," she was talking to the closed casket in front of her. "Every atom belonging to me belongs to you."

I felt kind of proud that she was my girlfriend and also thinking that it seemed like the wrong thought to be having at a time like that. But Samm was amazing up there in front of all these people who were there for David and who needed her to talk to them. When she was done, she stepped from behind the pulpit. She removed her cello from its case and took a seat in the middle of the stage. She slid her bow across the string one time and took a deep breath.

"I'm going to…"

Samm stopped talking and looked at her cello.

"This is Bach's Suite No. 1 in G," she said after a while. "David always asked me to play it for him. Before." And then she stopped again.

No one said anything. No one made a sound. Samm just sat there. We just waited. It was painful and beautiful at the same time. Take all the time you need, I thought, hoping she would know what I was thinking.

Play.

Don't play.

It's up to you, Samm.

Samm took several breaths. She slid her bow across the C string. At first, it was hardly audible; like she was not so much playing as calming herself. She rested her bow.

"David used to ask me to play this for him before he went to…"

Samm started again. "Before he went to Vietnam." Samm closed her eyes. Her fingers and hands and arms and cello became one. No one moved. No one made a sound. We all wanted to make sure David could hear every note.

• • •

We returned to school in the new decade, but it felt indistinguishable from the last one. The walk to school with Jonah, my classes, my teachers, the piles of homework. They were all the same. There were no revelations, no epiphanies, no satoris, not a single vision. Unless it was that nothing had changed. Not sure what I thought would be different, or wanted to change. But I was hoping for something to happen, some cosmic shift that would make life better.

But nothing changed.

Except Samm.

Samm was different. Bad different.

She didn't have much to say about anything. When she did talk, it was in a monotone and not her musical upbeat way that I loved to listen to. I tried to get her to come with me and do things, but she said she wasn't ready to go out and be with people. She said she wasn't mad at me. I tried to get her to let me come over. I even mailed her a letter. She thanked me for it, but she stayed quiet and distant.

The thing that worried me most was that she stopped playing her cello. Hadn't picked it up since she played the Bach piece for David in the church. Giving up music was too high a price for her to pay for what happened to David.

"You said Jews give up music for Shiva?" Samm asked.

"Yeah, but…"

"That's why I'm giving up music."

"You're not Jewish," I said.

"So what? Am I not good enough to follow a Jewish custom?"

"Not what I said."

"Not like you believe in god and you follow the rituals. All of a sudden, it's an exclusive club?"

"If I thought it would help, if I thought it was in any way good for you, I would say you're right. I'd agree with you and support you," I said. "But I don't think it will help at all. I think it's the opposite of helping you. It's just not good for you to stop making music. Especially now."

"And you are sure you know what will help me cope with David's suicide? What will help me understand why my brother killed himself."

"I do not." I felt like I was walking into things.

"Cello is that one thing that always makes me feel better," Samm said. "I'm not ready for that. I'm not ready to just feel better. I can't just play like nothing happened."

"I know."

"Then stop trying to get me to play."

"That's not what I meant."

"What do you care?"

"I care," I said.

"Then you should be supporting me, not telling me what to do."

"I'm not telling you what to do."

"You have no idea what I'm going through," she said.

"No, I don't."

"But you know what will make me feel better?"

"I don't know anything."

"Feeling better will mean I've moved on. That I've forgotten about David. Why would you want me to do that?"

That was when she hung up on me. And then she stopped taking my calls. I mailed her another letter, but she didn't reply or call me to even say she got it.

The thing is, I didn't disagree with her about any of it, and yet, I still wanted her to feel better. I knew that Samm had a legitimate reason to be depressed, and I knew that if she wasn't affected by David's death, it would be weird, but I also knew that being by herself was not the right thing to do. Maybe Shiva was a good ritual. I didn't know, but it seemed that being with people you know, people in your community, people who knew David, that was a way to return to the world. But I didn't know how to tell her because it was her brother who died. And he didn't only die.

Near the end of January, Samm called me.

"I want you to come with me on Saturday morning," she said.

"Okay."

"But I can't tell you where."

"I didn't ask."

"No. You didn't," Samm said. "I can't tell you."

"You don't have to."

"Really?" she said. Her voice sounded better.

"Samm, I believe the things you tell me and I don't care about what you don't. You must know that by now."

"I do."

"And I know you'll tell me more when you want to, or need to."

That Saturday morning I took the subway into the city and met Samm inside the 72nd Street station. That was when she told me that we were going to visit David.

"There's a reason I didn't tell you," Samm said.

"You don't need a reason."

"I didn't tell you because I wanted to go, but I wasn't sure I'd be able to follow through. And I didn't want any extra pressure in case I changed my mind."

"Okay."

"Okay."

We caught the Number 2 train up to the Bronx and walked the mile over to the cemetery. It was freezing. Colder than New Year's.

"Did you know Melville is buried here?" she said, as we entered through the cemetery gates.

"I did not."

"David grew grim about the mouth," Samm said quietly.

"What?"

"It's from *Moby Dick*."

"What does it mean?"

"He grew unhappy. Suicidal. Depressed." She pulled out a note with David's gravesite location, and we wove our way around the tiny street signs. "Did you know that Melville's kid committed suicide?" she said looking up. "He grew grim around the mouth."

"I did not know that. Is that meaningful?"

"No. It's merely a coincidence. I place little meaning on coincidences. Sometimes it seems like coincidences run our lives, but it's just randomness at work. We are too eager to let life be decided for us."

"I know that Melville wrote *Moby Dick* in a bar."

Samm laughed. "Odd segue."

"And he also never made money from writing."

"Yes. But he still felt that taking up the pen was his reason for living."

"Like the cello for you?"

"Irving Berlin," Samm said.

"What?"

"He's here too. This place has always had mixed company."

"Nondenominational."

"Also multiracial. From before it was widely accepted."

"Groundbreaking," I said.

"Almost not funny."

"Thank you. I'll be here all week."

Samm's family had been in New York for a while, and David was buried near a lot of their relatives. When we got to his grave, the ground was still barren. Samm sat on the cold ground next to David and began smoothing the dirt.

I wanted to give her a moment, so I drifted away in search of Melville who was supposed to be close by. All the shrubs and foliage were dormant, adding to the bleakness of the place. I stopped at a headstone and read the engraved quote:

"So we beat on, boats against the current, borne back ceaselessly into the past. The Great Gatsby"

I hadn't read Gatsby yet. It was on my English class reading list for April. I wasn't sure if constantly confronting the past was a good thing. I knew we needed to learn from history. But I didn't want to be ceaselessly pulled into my family's past. I didn't want Samm ceaselessly dragged back into reliving David's suicide. I wanted us to remember without reliving. We needed to create our own stories. New stories.

Samm called me, and I went to sit next to her. She leaned against me and we sat there, not talking. I was glad for her warmth.

"I made him come home," she said after a while.

"No, you didn't."

"If we hadn't looked for him, he'd still be alive."

"That's what you've been carrying around? You can't think that. It's just not true. He wanted to come home. He was happy to come home and be with his family. He wanted to be a kid again, at least for a while. He wanted to see your parents and he wanted to do Christmas with you. He loved you."

"How do you know?"

"I know," I said.

"How?"

"I just do." I pulled Samm closer, and we just sat there next to David.

"I know he's not here," she said. "Not actually here. But where is he? It's like death is an unknown country. Where do we go?"

"I don't think we go anywhere."

"It's not like I believe in any after life," Samm took a deep breath. "But I can't deal with the idea that David is just nothing. That he is nowhere."

"He's not nowhere. He's inside you. He's always going to be part of you. Memories are real. Thoughts are real. He's real."

"I wish I believed in a god. This might be easier. But it doesn't make any sense to think that there's a god, and it makes even less sense to think that if there is a god then that god gives a crap about any of us. Certainly he didn't give a crap about David or any of the guys in Vietnam." She paused for a moment. "I hate god."

"The one you don't believe in?"

"That one."

"I hate that god, too," I said.

"And I hate him, too."

"Who?"

"David," Samm said.

"I don't think you do."

"I do. For doing this."

"I get it," I said. "But I know you don't."

"I hate him for doing this. I'm worried that I will forget him because I hate him. Because he left me. And now I feel so alone," Samm said. "Why can't we save anybody?" she asked me.

"I don't know."

"We should be able to. If we're lucky someone saves us. Maybe we don't even know it while we're being saved. But not everyone gets saved."

"Maybe not everyone needs saving."

"Everyone needs saving."

"I need saving?" I said.

"You need saving."

"What do I need saving from?"

"Same thing everyone needs saving from."

"And what would that be?"

"Ourselves."

"Are you saving me?"

"Maybe we're saving each other," she said. And then she stopped talking, so I did too.

"Little things. Dull moments. They can save us," she added after several minutes. "Ordinary things. Ordinary moments. I always liked that story about Noah sending the dove out to test the water level."

"Yeah, I remember that."

"I like it because the dove is just an ordinary bird tasked with seeing if humans were ready to start over."

"A dove is ordinary?" I asked.

"It's a pigeon with better publicity."

I laughed. "You mean like a squirrel, which is just a rat with good PR."

"I know it's not true," Samm said.

"What?"

"I don't hate him."

"I know."

"It seems like no one else can understand how I feel. I know other people have loss. And I'm sure I don't understand how they feel."

"It's your loss and no one else's. It's okay to feel the way you feel."

"Isn't that a song?"

"It's because you love him, Samm," I said. "You're allowed to have your own grief. You're allowed to own it. It's okay to remember the pain. But you have to stop reliving it."

"My brother took care of me and I failed him. I keep thinking of that line from Hamlet how he was a fellow of infinite jest," Samm said. "David took care of me. He carried me. He held me up. He made me think I could do anything. And I believed him."

"He wasn't wrong. You can do anything."

"I'm lost. I'm empty and I can't do this." She started crying into my jacket.

"We'll do it together."

"I couldn't help him. I gave up on him. For some time I gave up on him. I'm not entitled to feel pain. To miss him."

"Of course you're entitled to miss him. And that doesn't have to be how you remember him. That's just your last memory. You have so many others. You need to pick other memories to hold onto."

"I keep thinking about this time when we were kids. We were in church and I had to fart the entire mass. I told David that the holy spirit helped me hold it in. David told me that maybe it was the holy spirit trying to get out. We laughed for a long time about that."

"He was crazy about you."

"You just said was." Samm sat up. "That was the first time you said was."

I felt bad. I didn't think. I just said it.

"He'll always be your brother."

"Everyone, my parents, they all tell me that I need to move on," Samm said. "I think everything should not move on. That's what I think should happen. It's an insult to David to want life to just go on. They want me to forget."

"No one wants you to forget. No one can make you forget. You don't have to say goodbye. But you do have to move on. Take him with you. Never forget," I said.

Samm didn't say anything.

"You look very tired," I said.

"I am very tired."

"When was the last time you slept?"

"I don't remember. I keep thinking that any country that can use its young for what it's doing is not one I want to be part of."

"Okay," I said, rubbing her back. We were going to freeze to death. "Where should we go?" I asked.

"You know that every fucking country in every fucking century has used up their young to fight wars. There's no fucking place to go. It's the world that I don't want to be part of."

"Then we may as well stay here?" I said.

"I'd like to go to Vienna," Samm said.

"Why Vienna?"

"They have those horses," Samm said.

"Okay, we'll go to Vienna."

"I miss him."

"Remember that list of stuff you don't believe in?" I said. "What do you believe in?"

"Nothing."

"What about UFOs?" I asked Samm. "Do you believe in those?"

"Those I believe in."

"Unicorns?"

"Absolutely real. And Santa. I'm sticking with Santa because I like presents and I don't care where they come from."

I kissed Samm. And then we started making out and I forgot how cold it was.

Samm jumped up. "Come on," she said and held out a gloveless hand which I took hold of. She started running, and I followed her lead. When we passed a new grave being dug, she stopped. The gravedigger didn't even look at us from his backhoe.

"That's his job," she said. "It's like on the one hand he's just digging holes in the ground. It seems so crude. But he takes care of the dead, and that seems so noble."

"I want to be cremated."

"Me too. But I'm scared of fire."

"Me too," I said.

"The cool thing about a cemetery is that everyone is the same here. We spend our whole lives trying to be different. Trying to get things and do things and go places and be somebody, but in the end, we all end up here. And everything is gone. And everyone is gone. Scares the shit out of me."

"You got to trust the things that scare you the most," I said.

"You're making my head hurt. Stop talking," she said and then started to run again.

We stopped by the bathroom and I loosened my grip on her hand, but she did not let go. Instead, she led me inside with her.

"How did you know it would be warm in here," I asked.

"I didn't." Samm pulled me into a stall and locked it. "For a smart guy you're sort of dumb," she said as she started opening my pants.

"Oh," I said, catching up. "Extremely dumb."

We pushed our clothes around and bared ourselves just enough to have sex in that tight space. I thought that Samm might be doing this for the wrong reason. But then I thought there was no wrong reason. Make love, not war. And then it was too late for me to think at all. I was committed.

We rearranged our clothes, and left the bathroom, walking calmly.

"You know how before I said I couldn't like you more?" I asked.

"Yeah."

"I lied."

"You lied to me?" Samm said.

"Yes. Because I already like you more now than when I said it. So I lied."

"You shouldn't lie to me."

"This was a special circumstance," I said.

"Very special."

"Are you ready to leave?"

"When did it get cold?" Samm said. "I'm fucking freezing."

"Is that a yes or a no? I can't tell."

"Yes," she laughed. "I'm hungry. I think there was a diner near the subway."

• • •

A woman was selling gloves and scarves and hats on 233rd Street, and Samm wanted to look. The woman was bundled up and wearing one of everything she sold.

Samm tried on one of her red plaid hats, the kind with ear flaps that fold down. Totally odd looking, but she looked so cute in it, and I told her so. She made me try one on. I was sure I didn't look as good as her. But that was always true.

"That looks so funny on you," she said. "Do you dare to eat a peach?"

"Not following, but I think it has to do with this hat."

"Prufrock."

"Okay," I said.

"Do you dare disturb the universe."

"As long as we can disturb it together."

"Then you must get that hat," she said. "We must both get them and wear them all day."

"Outstanding," I said. Samm was happy, and I liked that the hat was warming up my ears. They felt like icicles that could snap off at any moment.

We found a diner and stepped inside and looked around.

"Nuns," Samm nodded toward one of the booths. "That's a good sign."

"Why? Do they bless a place?"

"No, but they never go anywhere posh or dirty."

"Okay. We can sit?"

We drank coffee to warm up and waited for our food. Samm said we had to keep our hats on. I guess she meant she actually wanted us to wear them all day.

One of the nuns came over and told us she liked our hats. Then she asked us if we went to school nearby. We said we didn't, and Samm said we were visiting her brother at Woodlawn.

The other nun had joined her by then.

"Your brother," one said. "I'm sorry."

"He must be very young," the other said.

I looked at Samm to see if she was getting annoyed by the questions, but she looked happy to be telling them about David being a veteran and all. She left out the suicide. Said he died of complications from two tours in country. And the nuns also left out any questions about those complications that might have forced her to lie.

"Would you like us to pray with you?"

I was about to tell them I was Jewish, but Samm said yes.

The nuns sat in the booth with us and lowered their heads. Samm did the same.

"Dear Lord Jesus and Mary, Mother of God, hold your brave soul David in the palm of your hand, comfort him and his family and friends. Send angels of protection, love, and comfort to David's sister Samm. Send her the strength and courage to fulfill her destiny. We ask this through Christ our Lord. We ask all our prayers in Jesus' name. Amen."

"Amen," Samm responded.

"Amen," I said, following her lead.

"Thank you," Samm said as the nuns stood.

"You must forgive yourself," one of the nuns told Samm, and then they were gone.

Our food came, and we sat there not eating.

"Why would she say that?" Samm asked. "How did she know that?"

"I don't know. Maybe she didn't. Maybe we all need to forgive ourselves, like we all need to be saved. Maybe she says that to everyone who visits the cemetery, and then eats at this diner. Maybe we all blame ourselves when someone we love dies. I blamed myself for stuff when my grandfather died."

"Like what?"

"That I didn't spend enough time with him. That I didn't tell him how important he was to me. That kind of stuff."

"Let's eat," Samm said, popping the yolks on her eggs.

"Maybe they know that this war has a way of fucking with everyone," I said. I took a deep breath. "But mostly, maybe she could see it in your face."

Samm looked up from her home fries. "My face?"

"I love your face. But you look a bit shell shocked."

"I'm not trying to have a bad time," Samm said. "I'm just trying to avoid celebrating."

"After this, let's go downtown to Village Records and find some new music," I said. "I promise to make sure you don't enjoy yourself."

Samm laughed, and it was good to see her smile.

• • •

I pulled the door open and Samm slipped by me and we entered paradise. Inside were records lining every wall from floor to ceiling and bins of albums filled the floor space. The place was pretty crowded.

"That hat is too ugly for this store," Bob yelled at me as we passed the counter. "Well, your chick looks okay, but you can't wear it without looking ridiculous."

"I like how he looks in it," Samm said and then kissed me.

Bob was already talking to another customer. It was his store and he always seemed angry, though I was never sure he ever had anything to be angry about. And he insulted everyone, so it never seemed personal. And the guy knew everything about every kind of music. I liked listening to him debate customers about music. I learned a lot.

Samm showed me the new John Sebastian record. "The guy from Lovin' Spoonful," she said.

We were in the "S" section and I pulled out *Bridge Over Troubled Water*. I heard that Simon and Garfunkel skipped Woodstock to work on this."

"I wonder if they regret that," she said.

Samm was looking at the new Guess Who album. "I think I heard 'American Woman' on the radio," Samm said.

"Aren't they Canadians?"

"Awful joke," Samm said. "You're making sure I'm not having a good time?"

"That was funny." I pulled out the new Joan Baez record, *One Day at a Time*.

"Isn't that what alcoholics say?" Samm said.

"Yeah. But it's also how everyone gets through life."

"You're going to try to make this mean something about me being shell shocked?"

"Possibly."

"Why does everything have to have a meaning? I'm sick of symbolism. Why can't things be what they are?"

"Because things aren't anything. They have no meaning. People give things meaning."

"Okay," Samm said. "Can we go?"

"Why?"

"I feel like walking."

"Okay," I said. "Let me pay for this." I took *Bridge Over Troubled Water* to the counter and paid.

"That hat is a bold move, man," Bob said to me as he slipped the album into a bag.

I told Samm that the record was a present for her as we walked all the way to midtown along Sixth Avenue. When we reached 59th Street, we entered the park. There was a crowd by the pond, and as we got closer we saw that it was a large group of veterans. They must have been on some sort of field trip from the VA hospital. Many of the guys were in wheelchairs, others on crutches. The rest were walking without any assistance. They were with a number of nurses and aides who were moving around the group, ready to help. We stood and watched from a distance as they fed the ducks.

"Why would the ducks stay in the park when they could fly south for the winter?"

"They survive the winter by staying together," I said.

"More symbolism?"

"No, it's what they do."

"Well, it helps that people feed them." Samm started walking.

I followed as she led us north. I stopped to buy a pretzel, but she kept walking, and I ran to catch up and share the pretzel. It tasted pretty good; maybe I'd found my perfect pretzel. Or maybe it was just that I was cold again. Samm turned out of the Park onto 5th Avenue. As we neared the Metropolitan Museum she stopped by a homeless woman asking for spare change. Samm pulled out some dollar bills and dropped them into her cup. She removed her hat and offered it to the woman, who took it. Then she removed my hat, handed her that too, and started to walk again. When we reached the steps of the Met she raced me to the top. Except I dropped the record on the way up and it bounced down a few steps before someone picked it up and handed it to me.

I followed Samm inside. The rotunda was busy and we removed our jackets and I looked inside the bag and the record was shattered. I was going to throw it out, but Samm wanted to keep it.

"You can still get me a new one," she said as she scoured the floor until she found two valid entrance tickets which we waived as we walked past the guard.

"Is there something, in particular, you want to see?"

"Mummies."

We headed over toward the Egypt area and then down into the tombs.

"What we do for our dead," Samm said. "I think they removed all the organs before they did this."

"I don't know."

"It's just another dead person."

"But a fancy one," I said.

"Extremely fancy."

"You reconsidering mummification?"

After a few moments, Samm said, "I don't think we should talk about our deaths any more today."

"Earlier, when you said you didn't want to be part of the world, did you mean it?" I asked Samm when we climbed the steps out of the tomb.

"Do you think I'll kill myself like David?"

"No."

"Well, I do. I wonder if it's something we have in common. Something we both got from our parents mixing their genes. I wonder if I will do the same when things get hard for me. And they are hard now."

"Right now, this is happening. We are alive. That's all we can be sure of."

"Wow, underneath all that cynicism and despair and fear and ambivalence, you're an optimist," Samm said.

"Me?"

"It's okay, I won't tell anyone."

"That's not it. I'm not that much of an optimist."

"Then what?"

"I'm just not that smart."

"I've been having suicidal dreams," Samm said. "That's why I went to see David. I wanted him to tell me I would be okay."

"Did he?"

"There is no more David."

"Then I'll tell you." I stopped walking and Samm did too. "You're going to be okay."

"How do you know?"

"I don't know."

Jonah had told me that he and Lu were going to get dinner with Tony and Mel at the Sage Diner, and I told Samm we should meet them. She hadn't seen any of them since the funeral. Samm agreed, and we hopped on the subway. We switched trains at Grand Central, and as we waited for our train to Queens, I suggested that we could go upstairs and get railroad tickets to anywhere. Denver, San Francisco, Los Angeles. We could hit the road together.

"Love it. In search of Neil Cassidy," Samm said. "And it's exactly what I would want to do if I didn't think it would kill my parents to lose both their kids. That's how they would see it."

By the time we arrived, the others were seated at a booth. We joined them and Brucie came by and did his thing. Worth the meal right there. The diner had a TV on behind the counter, and Jonah and I turned to watch when we heard those four beautiful words, "pitchers and catchers report." The sports guy went on to show pictures of the Mets and Yankees Spring Training facilities. The new season was upon us. Hope was in the air. The slate was clean. And spring was on its way. We toasted each other.

"There is a lot seriously wrong with you guys," Lu laughed.

"They not only have issues," Tony said. "They are issues."

Samm showed everyone the album I bought for her and laughed as she told them how I broke it. Everyone laughed much harder than the story warranted.

After dinner, we went back to Tony's where we drank whiskey and ate Mel's homemade brownies. She had gotten good at baking them so that they were no longer crunchy. But they were still very potent.

Tony put on a Jefferson Airplane album.

"I love 'Greasy Heart,'" Samm jumped up. "Dance with me," she said, offering me her hand.

I got up and joined her. It was good to see Samm letting herself be happy. We danced for a while and then she put her arms around my neck.

"It's so weird to be both happy and sad at the same time," she whispered in my ear.

"Don't think about it," I told her. "At least not right now. Don't think at all."

ALL ALONG THE WATCHTOWER

All that running paid off, and I made the track team which promised to be a major focus of my spring. Jonah made varsity baseball. But he had a problem. The coach told him he had to cut his hair or be cut. At the end of practice, coach told Jonah he had until the weekend when he was penciled in to pitch the season opener. Jonah proclaimed the situation a mockery.

On Saturday, he tied his hair back and put on a turtleneck under his jersey. I arrived at the game after track practice. It was the top of the sixth, and Lu told me that Jonah had struck out ten and had yet to give up a hit. When a pitcher has a no-hitter going, no one comes near him in the dugout. That includes the coach. Jonah got three ground balls and took his seat by himself at the end of the bench. When he took the mound in the top of the seventh, the home crowd stood.

The first batter hit a grounder right back to the mound and Jonah threw him out. Then, the next batter tried to bunt, but our third baseman read the play and threw him out easily. The next batter took two strikes and then popped up to second. As the team mobbed Jonah, he threw his hat in the air and released his hair from under his turtleneck.

Back in the dugout he walked over to the coach and said, "I'm like Samson. I need the hair."

And that was the end of it. Mockery indeed.

• • •

Soon after the Mets opened their season, President Nixon announced that he was ordering the withdrawal of 150,000 troops from Vietnam. That seemed like good news. Even great news. Maybe the tide was turning. Maybe people had the power.

But Ali told me that everyone she knew was sure it was a smokescreen. It only took a few days until Nixon came back on television to prove her right. This time, he stood in front of color charts and maps to address the American people. We were being schooled like children as he sought to justify his decision to order US troops to invade Cambodia. He said that the North Vietnamese troops had long been using Cambodia as a sanctuary to launch deadly hit-and-run attacks on US troops in Vietnam. After they inflicted casualties on our troops, they would run back across the Cambodian border to the safety of their home bases, free from US retaliation.

No longer, he said.

Their aggression, he said, required a response from US troops who would now pursue their attackers into Cambodia.

Nixon was not winding the war down.

He was expanding it.

It didn't take long for protests to spring up all over college campuses. They seemed to have begun before his speech was done. Strikes were called. Classes canceled. Outrage and disruption were growing along with frustration.

I told Jonah that we had to do something.

He said he was tired of my obsession with a war I was powerless to alter. He didn't want to waste any more time talking about Vietnam. My obsession had not had any impact. Things were worse. He told me that this time there was no we.

"We don't vote. They don't care about kids. They don't even care about college students who do vote," Jonah said. "Why would they care about us? I'm done doing meaningless stuff."

"Let's do something meaningful," I said.

"I'm already doing lots of meaningful things," he said. "So are you."

It was true. Jonah was on varsity baseball and he was off to a great season and if he kept it up he had a good shot at playing college ball. Maybe even getting a scholarship. He told me he was pretty happy getting his school work done, playing baseball, and hanging out with Lu and the rest of us, and he didn't know why I couldn't be.

"You're on the track team," he said. "You got this amazing girl. We're both doing well in school so we can get into the same great college and do incredible stuff together when we graduate. Why can't you be happy with that?"

"You're right. But that doesn't make me wrong," I said.

"This is not your problem to fix," Jonah said. "Anyway, you can't fix this one."

"You can't ignore this either," I told Jonah.

"I'm not ignoring anything. I read the same articles you do. How does that do anything?"

It's not like I disagreed with Jonah. He wasn't wrong. But I needed to do something. I needed to do my part. It's just that I still wasn't sure what that was.

• • •

And then, on Monday, the fourth of May, during lunch, the news spread that 900 National Guardsmen had been sent to the campus of Kent State University in Ohio, and that the soldiers had opened fire on the students with live bullets.

Live bullets.

Several students had been killed and even more had been wounded.

Opened fire.

Our government had declared war on us. Our government had shot and killed unarmed students on a college campus. And the goddamned radio announcer was blaming the students for getting killed.

Students were shot in Ohio.

Four students were dead in Ohio.

I ran to Mr. Steel's room because I couldn't think of anything else to do. He had his radio out and was listening to reports. He motioned for me to sit. After a while, he said out loud, but not necessarily to me, that this changed everything. He just wasn't sure it would change anything for the better. Then he told me I should get to my next class.

I called Samm as soon as I got home, but there was no answer. Later, she called me from her school.

"Fucking Mondays," she said.

"I want to see you," I said.

Samm agreed to come to my house. I said I'd meet her on the platform at the Roosevelt station, and we'd come back together. I hung up and ran to the subway so I could get to Roosevelt first and be waiting when she got there. I didn't want her standing around by herself.

Samm arrived on the third E train. I was so happy to see her. To just see her. I didn't realize how much I had missed her even though I had seen her two days earlier. She walked over to where I was standing on the platform. I stood there for a moment, looking.

"What?" she said.

"Nothing."

"You're smiling."

"I'm happy to see you."

We hugged for a long time and waited for the Double G.

We'd been at my house about 15 minutes when Jonah, Lu, Tony, and Mel arrived and my mother fixed us trays of food and drink. We sat in my room, eating, talking, and listening to the radio. Everyone was trying to make sense out of the attack in Ohio. I called Ali every half hour.

Samm told us that some of her classmates wanted to organize a benefit concert to raise money for those injured in the shooting.

We brought the TV into my room and watched pictures from Kent State. On the radio, it was all anyone was talking about. It was the only thing we wanted to hear about.

My parents said it was okay if everyone slept over as long as they phoned their parents.

I wanted to find some alcohol. Jonah told me to raid the snack closet, too. Samm and Lu came with me to distract my mother while I searched the basement. I found an unopened bottle of scotch. Samm grabbed glasses from the kitchen and Lu took all the snacks she could carry.

"I'm glad I'm here," Samm said when we returned to my room. "I know it's funny, but this makes me miss David."

Tony poured everyone some scotch and offered a toast to David.

"To David," we all echoed.

Samm refilled everyone's glass. "To the students of Kent State," she said.

We spread sheets and blankets on the floor

I told them I wanted to organize a strike at school.

"We're sophomores," Lu said. "Not sure we know enough students to get them to follow us out of the building. We need the seniors."

"Are you saying Zach's not cool enough to shut the school down?" Tony said.

"Saying I think he is, but that not everyone else thinks that," Lu said.

"You're too nice," Mel said. "He's so not cool enough. It's why we love him."

"We should do something," I said.

"How would you do it?" Tony asked me. "How would you organize a strike?"

"We'd give a list of demands to the principal and then we'd march out of school and refuse to return to class until our demands were met. And we'd have a rally in front of the school and call the radio and TV stations and get some speakers."

"What demands?" Lu asked.

I pulled out a list I had written during school.

"You made a list?" Samm said.

"Lu is right," Mel said. "You are so uncool that you are cool."

"Read it to us," Jonah said.

"In light of the recent unprovoked shooting of US citizens by our own government, we, the students of Hills High, demand that the administration cancel all classes, hold a teach-in, condemn the war, and refuse to allow the military to recruit on school property."

"Nice," Jonah said. "Forget math, you should be a writer."

"Cancel classes?" Mel said. "I'm in."

"What would we need?" Tony asked.

"We'd need flyers. Maybe a thousand of them to let students know about the strike and what day and what period we planned on walking out of the school," I said. "We could hand them out before school and between classes."

"That's easy," Tony said. "What else?"

"We need students to follow us and walk out of the school," I said. "or we'll look like idiots."

"Won't be the first time," Jonah said.

"Some of us have had less practice than you," Samm laughed.

"Don't worry, Lu and I got this covered," Mel said.

"We do?" Lu said. "Covered how?"

"We get our girlfriends – in the bathroom, by phone – we get them to tell every chick they know that they need to show skin to help stop the war," Mel said. "Jonah, your sister, she could get like half the girls in school to go along with this," Mel added. "Short shorts, tank tops, halters. No bras. Summer time and dressing so fine and looking so pretty. Then we stand in the hallways when it's time to march out of school, and we tell the boys to follow us to the strike party."

"That's fucking genius," Jonah said. "Because we are that shallow."

"And because you are that sexy," Tony said, kissing Mel.

"I stopped listening after no bras," I said.

"Wendy could get the whole school to follow all by herself," Lu said. When no one said anything, she continued. "What? No one else thinks she's the prettiest girl in school? You must know this," she said to Jonah.

"She's my sister, so it's a little creepy," Jonah said.

"That's what I've been telling you," I said to Jonah.

"We all think that," Tony said. "We just liked hearing you say it."

"And she's also the scariest," Lu said. "No one would say no to her."

We talked for a while about the details, and when the conversation lost energy and no one said anything, each of us knew that we weren't going to be able to organize a strike.

I was glad they went along with it, even for a while. I was glad they did that for me.

"You truly are Don Quixote," Jonah said to me.

"Not by myself. You've always been right behind and next to me. Always."

"You know what freaks the shit out of me?" I said.

I poured everyone more scotch.

"I love riddles," Lu said.

"Everything?" Tony said.

"What if Woodstock was the end and not the beginning of change, of the revolution, of a new way? What if that was our best last moment? The coming together. The peace and love and happiness. Nothing funny about that. But, what if that was it? What if those three days was all we got? What if that was it?"

"That's a lot of what-ifs," Tony said.

"If the revolution did fail, well, then, I raise my glass to what a great dream it was," Samm said.

We poured shots and joined Samm in her toast.

• • •

I finally reached Ali on the phone around one in the morning. Columbia students were preparing to strike to shut down the college. Sal and Frankie and Sunny were meeting her on campus. I told her I wanted to join them. I asked everyone and told Ali we all wanted to come to Columbia and join the protest. We arranged a meeting place for the next day.

"Fearless and reckless," Ali said. "Fearless and reckless. For Grandpa."

I hung up the phone and decided that I should be able to be fearless with my friends. I told them all about my roof and how I went out there at night and how it was my Fortress of Solitude. And I told them that I had never told anyone about it. Not even Jonah.

I opened my window and we grabbed some joints. Jonah and Lu grabbed our glasses and Tony brought the scotch. We went out onto the shingles.

"Wow," Lu said. "I mean. Wow. Seriously."

"You rendered Lu speechless. That doesn't quite make you cool, but this roof does make you slightly less uncool," Jonah said.

"This is where I say, 'fuck you' to reality," I said.

"Reality is overrated," Samm said, hugging me.

"Reality needs an asshole every once in a while to keep it honest," Tony said, "And I am that asshole."

"You might or might not be that asshole," Mel said, "but you're my asshole."

"The stars are exceptional from up here," Lu said.

"Where do you suppose the last star is?" Samm asked. "And what do you suppose is after that? What is after the end of the universe?"

"I would love to go into space," Jonah said.

"You could if you wanted to," Lu told him.

"You know," Tony said. "It's not like we actually go into space. I mean, we live in space. We're just exploring our neighborhood."

I poured everyone the last of the scotch and told them to wait to drink it because I had one more toast.

"Someone stop him before it's too late," Jonah said.

"It's already too late," Tony said.

I stood on the shingles and steadied myself. "Samm, Jonah, Tony, Mel, Lu," I said. "I raise my glass to our friendship. Friendship is outstanding. Friendship is just fucking weird. We pick another human being, a stranger, and we think, yeah, I like this one. And then we do stuff with them. And we don't have to and they don't have to. There's just absolutely no reason to have each other's back, to be there for each other. There's no blood tie or the promise of sex. Together we have become a makeshift family. We gather around each other and that lets us…that gives us more strength to face the battering we get from the world around us. It's a beautiful thing and it makes me happy. It makes me proud and I am honored to share friendship and family with each of you."

We emptied our cups and I sat back down. Samm kissed me and squeezed my hand.

"Someday," Tony said, "we'll look back and remember this moment in time with satisfaction and with happiness."

"And we'll look back on it together," Mel said.

"No way we remember any of this," Jonah said. "At least not the way it happened."

"But that's just it," I said. I thought about it for a moment and added, "This isn't over yet."

Elan Barnehama is an author and teacher. He was born in Manhattan and grew up in Queens. He has a BA from Binghamton and an MFA from the University of Massachusetts, Amherst. His fiction and nonfiction have appeared in numerous publications and on public radio. He has taught writing and served as a fiction editor and ghostwriter. He coached high school varsity baseball, had a gig as a radio news guy, and did a mediocre job as a short-order cook. He's a New Yorker by geography. A Mets fan by default. *ESCAPE ROUTE* is his second novel.

Photo credit Rhonda Fishman

Past Titles

Running Wild Stories Anthology, Volume 1
Running Wild Anthology of Novellas, Volume 1
Jersey Diner by Lisa Diane Kastner
The Kidnapped by Dwight L. Wilson
Running Wild Stories Anthology, Volume 2
Running Wild Novella Anthology, Volume 2, Part 1
Running Wild Novella Anthology, Volume 2, Part 2
Running Wild Stories Anthology, Volume 3
Running Wild's Best of 2017, AWP Special Edition
Running Wild's Best of 2018
Build Your Music Career From Scratch, Second Edition by Andrae Alexander
Writers Resist: Anthology 2018 with featured editors Sara Marchant and Kit-Bacon Gressitt
Frontal Matter: Glue Gone Wild by Suzanne Samples
Mickey: The Giveaway Boy by Robert M. Shafer
Dark Corners by Reuben "Tihi" Hayslett
The Resistors by Dwight L. Wilson
Open My Eyes by Tommy Hahn
Legendary by Amelia Kibbie
Christine, Released by E. Burke
Running Wild Stories Anthology, Volume 4
Tough Love at Mystic Bay by Elizabeth Sowden
The Faith Machine by Tone Milazzo
The Newly Tattooed's Guide to Aftercare by Aliza Dube
American Cycle by Larry Beckett
Magpie's Return by Curtis Smith
Gaijin by Sarah Z. Sleeper
Recon: The Trilogy + 1 by Ben White
Sodom & Gomorrah on a Saturday Night by Christa Miller

Upcoming Titles

Running Wild Novella Anthology, Volume 4
Antlers of Bone by Taylor Sowden
Blue Woman/Burning Woman by Lale Davidson
Something Is Better than Nothing by Alicia Barksdale
Take Me With You By Vanessa Carlisle
Mickey: Surviving Salvation by Robert Shafer
Running Wild Anthology of Stories, Volume 5 by Various
Running Wild Novella Anthology, Volume 5 by Various
Whales Swim Naked by Eric Gethers
Stargazing in Solitude by Suzanne Samples
American Cycle by Larry Beckett

Running Wild Press publishes stories that cross genres with great stories and writing. RIZE publishes great genre stories written by people of color and by authors who identify with other marginalized groups. Our team consists of:

Lisa Diane Kastner, Founder and Executive Editor
Andrea Johnson, Acquisitions Editor, RIZE
Rebecca Dimyan, Editor
Andrew DiPrinzio, Editor
Cecilia Kennedy, Editor
Barbara Lockwood, Editor
Chris Major, Editor
Cody Sisco, Editor
Chih Wang, Editor
Benjamin White, Editor
Peter A. Wright, Editor
Lisa Montagne, Director of Education
Pulp Art Studios, Cover Design
Standout Books, Interior Design
Polgarus Studios, Interior Design
Nicole Tiskus, Production Manager
Alex Riklin, Production Manager
Alexis August, Production Manager
Priya Raman-Bogan, Social Media Manager

Learn more about us and our stories at www.runningwildpress.com

Loved this story and want more? Follow us at www.runningwildpress.com, www.facebook/runningwildpress, on Twitter @lisadkastner @RunWildBooks

RUNNING

Wild

PRESS